"For the love of God, Montresor!"

— Edgar Allen Poe, *The Cask of Amontillado* —

CASK

THE NOVEL

CASK

THE NOVEL

FARLEY L. DUNN

◆◆◆ THREE SKILLET

Published in Fort Worth, Texas

 THREE SKILLET

www.ThreeSkilletPublishing.com

Three Skillet Publishing
PO Box 162194
Fort Worth, Texas 76161

Cask originally appeared as a novella in *The Electric Minute, Vol. 5*, a short story collection.

ISBN: 978-1-943189-89-2

Second Printing May 2021/ Printed in the USA

Table of Contents

—Chapter 1—

Interstellar Ranger *Franklin Delano Roosevelt*

Captain Vicente Falco
. . . who enjoys a bit of late-night conversation

THE SHIP BREATHED its last dying breaths in the harsh, acrid smoke billowing from under the main navigation array as the screens across my console went dark. Then the entire Bridge plunged into midnight.

I breathed a sigh of relief as I removed my Virtual mask, even as my heart pounded. No light on the real Bridge, either. It wasn't too bad. At least we were "on world," and the screeching of torn metal and whistling wind was silenced. My face was sore where the mask had twisted in the crash. I wondered who else had survived. I took a deep breath and put that aside. Clearly the *Roosevelt* wasn't heading back into space without a few minor repairs . . . make that major retrofits from bow to stern. I was forced to admit to myself, the old *F.D.R.* probably wasn't heading anywhere this side of the next century. Two decades we'd been together, the last five years with me as her Captain. I'd miss the old girl.

I counted off the seconds in my head. Forty-four . . . forty-five, and with a buzzing sound, red lights along the floor flickered and came to life. Two hours. That's the battery backup for the emergency lighting. Any longer was unnecessary. If you're dead longer than two hours in space, you don't need light. You're really and truly dead.

I pulled myself off the floor and shook, mostly to check out my joints. I felt good, nearly a hundred percent. Better than I could expect for landing on this hellish world. First our instruments had begun fluctuating wildly, despite being fully shielded, then it was like we'd been grabbed by a fist and yanked through a hundred kilometers of atmosphere and flung to the ground.

"Song?" I called my First Mate's name. Jiang Song was my perfect foil, with a quick wit, able to throw humorous barbs at me to make her point, yet not alienate me in the process. She was a good woman to have around. Of course, having a dark-haired beauty like Jiang as my second wasn't to be sniffled at hormonally, either. I could do worse, and in fact had. I hoped she'd survived. By all that was out there, I hoped the woman was still alive.

"Sir! Captain Falco!" The words were muffled,

but they sounded like they were from the lift.

"Yeah! Is that you, Sister?" Sister is our Engineer, Sanaa Nakato Ssanyu. We call her Sister because we can't always determine which of her personalities is currently dominate. A split-personality construct engineered from an African genetic database, no one wants to offend the wrong sister. Sanaa, the dominate one, has an aggressive streak, a bulldog attitude that refuses to let go of a problem once it's in her leash range. Perfect for an Interstellar Ranger like the *Roosevelt*. My Sister (Sanaa's name for her primary personality) is her kinder twin, the original sister, the one who knows how to show compassion, recognizing that a life is unrecoverable, or a ship will no longer fly. I hoped Sanaa was on the other side of that door.

"Sir, power's out. I'll have this door open in another minute."

"I'm your number one man, Sister." Now that I knew who I was talking with, I felt better. If anyone could make sense of this mess, Sanaa could.

"You just take care of Jiang. I want to find her alive when I get this door open." Banging noises accompanied the words.

Yeah, so do I, I thought, but I took a deep breath instead of saying the words. At Song's console, I saw a leg protruding from underneath.

"Song?" I knelt and grasped the ankle. It was

warm, still, so she was either alive or recently dead. I couldn't consider the second and dismissed it immediately. "Jiang, it's Falco. Sister's at the lift. I need your help."

The leg stirred, and I sighed in relief. I had dismissed the second possibility, but I was as pragmatic as they come. A captain needs pragmatism. Or a My Sister, to tell her Captain when a life is unrecoverable or a ship will no longer fly. Even when we couldn't see her, My Sister was somewhere behind those eyes, hidden beneath Sanaa's aggressive personality.

"At least one of us is up and at 'em." The leg pulled away, and Song appeared, her straight black hair gleaming in the dull red light. She pushed it from her face, pulling herself to her seat, with a smirk on her red lips. "A landing like that could bruise a girl. Next time just tell me you'd like some rough-and-tumble. There are better ways."

I sat and put my hand on my forehead, surprised to find it damp with concern. Maybe I hadn't dismissed the second at all. Maybe I'd really been worried. I knew I was relieved.

"You think the Envoy's a little shook up?" Song tapped at her console, finally slapping her palm against its surface when there was no response.

"An hour and three quarters, and we need to be out of this vessel." I pulled myself up. I hoped the

CASK

Envoy wasn't too shook up, to quote that old song. Elvis, from the twentieth century. Hey, I'm still a fan, and Song has no compunctions about teasing me unmercifully. I'm sure I deserve it, but the man was the original rocker. Who can discount that?

The Envoy was our mission. Was. Would still be if we could jerry-rig enough power to get a rescue beacon out via the Android. The shiplink would need to be undamaged, but I was certain Sanaa would have no trouble dealing with that. She was the best ship's engineer between here and Earth. Perhaps the only one.

"There!" The word vomited into the reddened air as the lift doors whined and snapped back. The interior glowed crimson as did the rest of the Bridge. Sanaa (clearly still in control) pulled herself up three feet—that didn't look right—and tossed aside a metal bar much like an old crowbar. "Lift's out of alignment, but that's the good news. It's going to take more than a socket wrench to put the rest of this bucket back together. Anyone for a hike to," and she paused, "St. Petersburg?"

I caught the look. As Engineer, Sanaa had corneal inserts that served as full imagers. That way she carried ship's diagrams with her, freeing up her hands for more useful endeavors, like breaking through stuck lift doors.

"Russia?" Song laughed. Her fingers idly tapped at her console, as if it might respond, if she gave it a chance. "As if. We didn't get anywhere close to Earth. Sorry, Sister. Maybe in about five hundred light years."

"As the crow flies." I chuckled. St. Petersburg was an outpost, a colony that had been thought lost for over a hundred years. Their ship had reported massive guidance system failures before all communication was lost. The mission landed on this world, Verboten, hidden by its massive magnetic field, until rediscovered about a decade ago. They were our hope for rescue. "Is our Envoy still green?"

The Envoy was our stab at averting an interstellar war that threatened to consume Earth's faltering population, and perhaps decimate the first truly intelligent alien lifeform we'd come across. If the Envoy was lost, there wasn't much point in all the rest.

"Don't know." Sanaa had pulled a wall panel free, and she was tripping connections. She yanked a wire and snorted when it came free in her hand. She reached inside, pulled a tool from a pocket, worked with it, and reset the connections. Fans under the consoles whirred, the lights in the room flickered, sizzled, then went dark again. The emergencies were off, and we waited. I didn't get to forty-five, because popping noises came from inside the wall panel, and it burst into flames at about count fifteen, quickly eating into the rest of the wall.

The localized fire suppressants didn't trigger on.

"That's not good." Sanaa backed away, tossing the small tool to the side.

"Can we exit via the lift?" I planned to, regardless. Burn alive? Not my idea of a good time. There was a maintenance hatch in the ceiling, but I didn't remember it leading to an outside access panel. Smoke was filling the Bridge, and Song began to cough.

"Yes, sir, if you don't mind shimmying through the bottom half of the opening to the level below. Song, are you injured?" Sanaa knelt at Song's side, taking her hand. With that, I knew My Sister had assumed control. She was the subordinate personality of the construct, but she was also the first twin. She had control, when she chose to take it. She usually relinquished to her sibling. The concern she felt must be strong for her to step in. Perhaps Song wasn't disclosing everything.

"Not a scratch." Song stood, rifling through the tray at the front of her console. In the flickering light of the flames, I was surprised she could see anything. Besides, I was already at the lift.

"Out, everyone. Song, leave that and get over here." In addition to the flames, the big ship was settling, and the metal parts of the vessel groaned with the stresses of being on a planet with heavier than normal gravity. That spoke of the damage she'd taken. She was sturdy as a Jovian CloudSkipper. The fall must have broken her keel. That crushed my heart, but there was nothing I could do about that here and now, except try to get out alive. The problem? The Captain must be last off the ship, and Song was digging through her personal junk. Come on, Song!

The flames must have been eating at something behind the panels. Tongues of fire leaped out of a grille across the room, creating a cacophonous dance of ever-increasing incandescent fury. I yelled, "Song, now!"

She took another minute, frantically pawing, before knocking several items to the floor; and snatching one up, she forced it into a pocket, as she ran my way. We hit the floor of the lift in a tumble. The bottom half of the doorway was a black maw leading to whatever damage was hidden below.

"At least the lower level's not on fire," I joked.

"That's the least of our worries." Clearly, Sanaa had resumed dominance. "Like I said, this lift? This is the good news."

"What did they used to say about Elvis?" Song had her feet already through the pitch-black opening. "Not the fat part, the other thing."

I caught her eye, and she was grinning. I thought, with a frown, and I shrugged.

"Elvis has left the building." She laughed and

CASK

disappeared into the darkness.

"And you picked her for your First Mate?" Sanaa snorted and disappeared after her.

"At least I don't lack for good conversation," I called after her. Then the Bridge exploded into flames, and I dove through headfirst, not caring what I found on the other side.

—Chapter 2—

Dreadnaught *Vladimir Vladimirovich Putin*

Mission Commander Tayari Tesfaye
. . . in which the curtain rises on a new cast

"I BELIEVE I CAN OFFER a point we can all agree on."

Mission Commander Tayari Tesfaye, his barrel chest boasting a leopard-skin sash, stood on the Bridge of the *Vladimir Putin* and jockeyed for the command of a battleground that was about to devolve into bloodshed and annihilation.

The dreadnaught was in full pursuit of the *F.D.R.*, and opinions on what would happen if and when they located her had erupted in near violence. "If," on Tesfaye's one hand, was from Captain Kalinda Devi, with her, "Here's what we want to do," soliloquies, and the "when" on Tesfaye's other hand had erupted from General Arminius Agrippa, a virulent lightning bolt erupting from a man boasting folded leather for a face and steel-gray hair holding it to his skull.

"Get my military team on this Bridge, and that ship will be ours. Mark my words." Agrippa punched his demand with a balled fist, as he twisted it upwards at chest level. He was a man who cut his words into brittle shards, with no room for excess or buttery phrases. Burned was better than buttered, and you could like it or get out of his way. A snort from deep inside his throat told the finality of his thoughts on the matter.

"Now, General," Tesfaye smoothed, "I have no doubts your team would be perfectly capable, and possibly more experienced at this type of pursuit—"

"Finally, someone's listening." Agrippa cut his eyes to Captain Devi, his face erupting into full gloat.

"—but this is the Captain's ship, and we must concede the Bridge to her and her crew."

Tesfaye knew he was fudging the moment in Devi's favor, as she was only nominally in control of the Bridge. Even so, as Mission Commander, responsible for the behavior and actions of both the General and the Captain but with limited control of either, he intended to weave this situation into a four-layered gabi he could proudly wear when he returned as an old man to his native Ethiopia.

"Thank you, Commander," Captain Devi offered in peacekeeping, as she touched the tip of a delicate finger to a brilliant red ruby catching the light to one side of her nose. "What is the point you would wish to offer us? I will be pleased to listen if the General will hold his words while you speak."

First Helmsman Azizi Quispe, with dark eyes that reflected his Inca extraction, paused his hands at his control board and turned his head just enough to catch Devi's eye. Devi gave an almost imperceptible nod, and a smile ghosted Quispe's face as he turned back to his assigned task.

Clearly, the crew of the *V.V.P.* felt solidarity in the face of the bull-run heavy handedness thrashed about by the General. At least the Army crew—those brought on board specifically for this mission and answerable only to General Agrippa—were content to keep to their part of the ship, even though "their part of the ship" had been the Navy crew's off-duty and recreation area only weeks ago. That sucked, but it would suck worse if they had to intermingle with them on an hourly basis.

"Anytime you want to start," Agrippa barked, giving his attention to the braiding on his cuff. Making sure his attention was anywhere but on the Mission Commander and the Captain thickened the air on the Bridge until it could be cut with a knife.

"Yes." Tesfaye took in a deep breath and held it for a moment before releasing it. He looked at the Captain, her dark eyes on him and one hand kneading the prayer cloth she continually carried. It was a sign of her Indian faith and revealed her view of the world: that to better oneself in this lifetime was to receive a higher place in the next. He nodded, and he took a moment to assess the General, considering whether he would really listen or ignore him as he usually did.

It was out of his hand, nonetheless. The Captain, she would listen politely, but if she disagreed with him—which was often—she would do what she wanted, anyway. The General was apt to stamp away to the safely of his military team, a high-tech and highly modified cadre of hand-picked soldiers specially selected to ensure the success of this mission.

And that didn't count the 300 infantrymen from the vats of the military's clone factories. They remained in the ship's Stasis Barracks until the *F.D.R.* was in their ship's sights.

Tesfaye broke the silence, saying, "This will be easier, Captain, if we speak in private."

"If that is what you wish." Devi stood, and she called out to the crew on the Bridge, "If you will please, for a moment, step outside, I will appreciate it." She turned to Tesfaye. "A moment is enough, I assume."

Tesfaye nodded. Devi had made her point. She would give in because he was the Mission Commander, but only just. This was her bridge, and she—and only she—commanded it. Around them, twelve people stood, eerily silent, and moved toward the lifts, two on either side of the room.

Tesfaye noted each crewman. Helmsman Quispe, who had caught Devi's eyes earlier. He waited on two others, First Mate and Executive Officer August Murphy, a massively muscular man standing well over two meters spattered with red freckles on his arms and into his hairline who had just arrived on the Bridge to take the first watchshift; and Navigator Edwige John, a tiny woman with a thick tangle of hair wearing jewel tone nails. John pumped her hips as she walked, something Tesfaye had observed on other occasions, and he wondered if it was natural or purposeful.

First Engineer Manu Rodriguez had arrived with Murphy, although they hadn't seemed to be together. Rodriguez, the graybeard of the team, had moved to Kai Kumar's side and begun a vigorous conversation. Kumar, his bulk straining his clothing, was the Sensors Calibration & Flight Command Systems Technician. The two exited together, with Kumar out of breath before he got to the door.

Ship's Purser Ginevra Yilmaz had clearly been on the Bridge for no other reason than to attract Azizi Quispe's attention, but there had been no spark that Tesfaye had seen. She had left a small gift at Quispe's elbow, which he had furtively raked into a shallow drawer. Loadmaster Josiah Peeters, whom Tesfaye unequivocally knew ran a surreptitious black market on restricted goods from ship's stores, palmed and pocketed something from Communication Systems Technician Dasha Ivanova, who was running scans on a screen with Information Systems Technician Soren Hansen, a man who knew seven languages and could double up at Ivanova's job in a pinch. All four were on one side of the Bridge and made their way to the same lift.

The final three were Data Collection Technician Ziggy Korhonen, who bore an uncanny resemblance to Soren Hansen; Third Engineer Saskia Kazlauskas, who tripped a breaker, leaving a bank of lights in the dark; and Second Engineer Lilou Apinelu, who patted Kazlauskas on the shoulder and collected a glass tablet on the way out.

Eerie was an understatement, Tesfaye decided. The exit had felt near to rehearsed in its silence and smoothness. He was unsure why some of them had been in attendance, except that it was well-known that Agrippa and Devi could barely work together, and sparks were likely to fly when they gathered on the Bridge.

A fireworks show in space, how about that! Tesfaye had to concede one thing: This mission had turned out to be anything but boring.

He could use a little boring, especially as he felt the day was about to get much worse.

CASK

—Chapter 3—

Interstellar Ranger *Franklin Delano Roosevelt*

Science Officer Aldrik Jollenbeck
. . . in which wheels make a difference

ALDRIK JOLLENBECK considered his options:

One, I can sit and do nothing. Wait for help, maybe. See what Captain Falco intends to do. Hope the power is restored.

Two, I can figure out a way to get out of this mess. Keep trying to access the mainframe. Upload a signal. Download answers. Put my brilliant reputation to the test and prove I'm as smart as I claim I am.

On second thought, he chuckled, only one of those two options is viable. So, what can I do?

Mainframe, inaccessible. The Holo-Lab is evidence of that.

Globular Cluster Gene Inversion trial, toast. Two hours in the Holo-Lab lost. There wasn't time for the system to back up the information. Likely the rest is fried as well. Four months of work, all ready to harvest, now gone.

Vision, unsure. With ship's power down, the darkness is so complete, even my most sensitive optics aren't pulling in images. My LiDAR is up and fully functioning, however. That tells me exactly where I am, and that I'm alone. I expected that, so it's no surprise.

Communication, sluggish. Only that one access point when the lights flashed on for a moment, allowing me to grab a full Dump. It's got to wait.

Jollenbeck's focus shifted outside himself as he pushed it aside, leaving the Data Dump in standby, its red icon blinking.

Chair, he didn't know. He thought for a moment and ran several options through his mind.

Testing the magnetic lift, he felt movement, and his LiDAR imagery indicated increased elevation. Port thruster? He tapped once, at minimal, and LiDAR confirmed the change in yaw. It was so minute he hardly felt it, but the sensors were based in science. Any change, no matter how minute, was a change. Starboard performed identically, and he breathed a sigh of relief, if he could be said to breathe at all.

Medical Officer Richard Franklin had been in the Holo-Lab with him when the circuits seized, holding an old-fashioned beaker, and pouring a solution into a graduated cylinder for analysis.

Jollenbeck's favorite among the crew, Franklin often joined him, aiding him in his passion for research and the ensuing results he obtained. Pure information. That's what drove Jollenbeck. Pure information, from any source.

Now, he felt trapped, no, *was* trapped, unable to move his arms, his legs, or his mind. He'd go crazy if he couldn't interact with the world.

Patience. Think it through, Jolley. There is no situation in which rational thought cannot achieve the desired end, if only I concentrate on the immediate problem.

He perused the facts: The mainframe is down; I have vision, but only through LiDAR; I can't contact anyone. On the positive side, the Data Dump might have answers; I do have functioning LiDAR; and I'm mobile.

He ran a power check. With the ship systems down, inductive charging was offline. His internal Tesla reactor had been giving low CED readings since his chair's last retrofit. As even his lowly crewmates knew, anytime the Central Electron Density along the Tokamak Axis dropped, total energy output was, by simple extrapolation, compromised. Battery storage became paramount.

It hadn't been a problem with ship's inductive charging capabilities continually topping off his reserves. Now? At least, across the board, lights were green on all batteries. If his Tesla went fully offline also, he could manage fourteen hours at full draw. If he was careful, tweaking the Energy Confinement Time, he might be able to stretch that to a full day. The Tesla allowed him to operate indefinitely under optimal conditions.

Low CED outputs were not optimal. No power slides for me, he thought with a dry twist. He wanted to chuckle but refused to engage his Assist. The Aakash interactive AI pulled power, and it was power he didn't have to spare, at least until the ship came back online.

Anyway, there was no one to hear.

With power offline, he mused, I can't exit the room. Doors are also offline, meaning I must wait. That gives me time. To? That's obvious, the only thing I can do.

He reached to the Data Dump and cracked it like an egg against the side of a pan. Careful not to let it spill, he pulled a portion of the shell away, studying the glowing layers of data fabric inside, like the yolk and its albumen, one trying but not quite managing to obscure the other. Running a virtual pointer down the layers, one leaped out, screaming.

"Caution, Caution, Impending Impact!"

The words blinked in a vibrant, neon twinkle, insisting, Read Me, Read Me! He adjusted the virtual pointer, probed the urgent section, and the words flooded through the crack in the shell to fill the visible sphere of his internal world.

He reached for the accompanying words, touched and absorbed them.

"Reverse thrusters fully engaged . . ."

"Distress beacon Charlie Alpha Three, Interstellar Ranger *Franklin Delano Roosevelt*, repeat, Interstellar Ranger *Franklin Delano Roosevelt* going down . . ."

"Within scanning range of Verboten; no life signs registering . . ."

No life signs? St. Petersburg was fully functional as an outpost settlement. True, they had no trading commodities to entice others to visit, and the massive magnetic fields were a barrier that only the most intrepid of captains—or the most stupid—tried to navigate, plus nine decades of isolation had skewed their society into isolationism. However, in an attempt to break free of that, they'd recently signed an agreement with Daimler-Porsche, the maker of his Aakash, to operate as a planet-based "space dock" for travelers in need of supplies or repairs, in the hopes, on Daimler-Porsche's side, that they could one day monopolize any resources discovered on the planet.

Daimler-Porsche's investment in the settlement said the Dump couldn't be correct. They would protect their investment, and that meant protecting the people who maintained their space-side access points. That meant protecting St. Petersburg.

It was irrelevant at this time, so he tossed it aside, and the words collapsed around him into a small cache at his side. Probing deeper into the Dump, he pulled the shell wider, looking for what his very busy shipboard companions were occupied with just before the breach in power.

Before the *crash*.

Surely this had been a crash, a full, planet-based landing, one done unexpectedly and in a blindingly hasty manner. Nothing else could have triggered a full shutdown of ship's power.

The crew's files glittered like fireflies, waiting to be captured. He reached for them greedily, only to have them skitter out of his reach.

Oh, elusive little things. Never you mind. He tensed his entire being, shuddered with the effort, and sent out a Sticky Probe, snagging the first one.

Falco, Vicente, Captain: On the Bridge, as he expected, fully engaged in monitoring the ship. He was a man with little tolerance for mistakes, hence Jollenbeck's ongoing curiosity about his relationship with his First Mate. It was none of the Science Officer's business, however, and he determined once again to pry no more than necessary for the functional capability of the ship and crew.

Song, Jiang, First Mate: Also engaged on the Bridge, although not in virtual as the Captain had been. Song's electronic interactions were smooth, if terse, until the data stream ended in a violent flash of optic-quality gibberish. Just before the gibberish blasted the system, in a crude joke written but not sent, Song's tendency to barb people with irascible humor to make her point came across as a painfully bright, red flash, tagged by the system to be deleted. It seemed Song hadn't been quick enough to outwit the ship's Morality Decryption Sensors. Hey, each to his own. She rarely heckled him, so it was none of his business. He considered that the Decryption Sensors' reaction to the joke could account for the gibberish, perhaps even for the ship being powered down, but he suspected it was something far more sinister.

Franklin, Richard, Medical Officer: Richard and he had been in the Holo-Lab together. A friendly man to everyone on the crew—and the easiest of the group to get along with—he and Jollenbeck had bonded early on. He'd trust Franklin in any situation. Jollenbeck was surprised to discover the man had a virtual SkinFlick running in the background as they worked in the lab. How amusing! He'd not have thought that of Franklin. Yet, there was nothing ominous in the medical officer's data stream, and he moved on.

As a good science officer, Jollenbeck considered himself in his mental list. His records were in the Data Dump, also. He'd been with Franklin, even if they were in completely different locations within the ship. He probed each part of himself that had been in contact with ship's systems at the time of the breach. His chair had been in full operational mode, from the induction charging to his Aakash Assist, seamlessly collecting Jollenbeck's every thought, and interpreting each one for transmission to the outside world. He found no conflicts, no red flags, and nothing to think he'd been compromised at the time.

Ssanyu, Sanaa Nakato, Engineer: Wildly erratic, in Jollenbeck's estimation. As a scientist, he preferred things in boxes, neatly studied, tallied, and stored away in an orderly fashion. Ssanyu was anything but. You never knew who you were speaking with from moment to moment. The dominate twin was Sanaa, but My Sister often appeared without warning. More than once, he'd embarrassed himself with an electronic, Assist-shared joke, only to find that he was speaking with the wrong twin. Even so, the Dump suggested it was the good Engineer who had been the first to recognize there was a potential problem. Sister—even Jollenbeck used the label as a generic reference—had been frantically attempting to intervene in the impending crash for some minutes before the rest of the crew knew anything was amiss. Jollenbeck scanned her attempts and could find nothing wrong with ship's systems. The craft had simply gone down, with no apparent cause.

Army Support Personnel Cpt. Xavier Hernandez, Lt. Keenan McAvoy, and Lt. Nikolaus Nissen, aka Ghost, Recon, and Pyro: Jollenbeck skimmed the three men with little sense of finding anything. Ghost's interactive link had been in sleep mode at the time of the power down. The trio maintained one bunk and kept a schedule of two awake and one resting at all times. Recon and Pyro had been involved in a virtual gaming session: Ghost Recon, Cygnus Edition. No one on board the ship questioned where the men had gotten their rather unimaginative handles: the Game. It was the latest platform and designed to take full advantage of the current tensions between the Cygnians and Humanity. The game's tagline: Humanity's Fist Crushes the Cygnian Hordes. The game was of no interest to Jollenbeck, and he moved on.

Zubizarreta, Silvestre, Bishop: Jollenbeck automatically grouped the Bishop with his acolyte. They were paired in a way only the devoutly religious could be. They were along to satisfy the Religious Right to Unity's demands that Humanity's moral and religious side be represented on the Envoy's long journey. Jollenbeck saw the truth of the matter. Zubizarreta was aboard to proselytize the alien Envoy. The Acolyte—he had no other name—was a youth who mimicked his master so closely that if one stood between them, it was possible to have a conversation with the replies returned in stereophonic clarity. The two were involved in a religious exercise at the time of the breach, saying prayers to their god through the ship's virtual Talisman of Holy Entreaties.

Android: The mobile control nexus of the ship, the Android was everywhere. Jollenbeck found traces of digital Android-ness no matter where he looked. He expected no less. The Android *was* the ship, fully capable, and integrated down to the last carbon neuron. Comprised of a malleable shape around a reconfigurable titanium-alloy framework, the Android was whatever the crew needed it to be. From male deckhand to female companion, there was no end to its uses. At the time of the breach, the Android had been in the ship's Nexus Hub, physically attached to thirty-six datapoints, the most into which its design parameters allowed it to fracture. Jollenbeck cringed. He trusted the Android had survived the severing of so many connections at once. If so, he hoped it was still sane.

Envoy: The Envoy was more difficult to assess. Jollenbeck had to negotiate with the Cask's AI to find out much at all, and as communications were down, that wasn't happening soon. The Cygnian diplomat was kept in near-stasis to dilute the effects of the trip aboard the lower-gravity vessel preferred by Humanity. Its Cask-standard AI was nowhere near Jollenbeck's Assist's level of sentience, only designed to funnel information to the near-vegetative Envoy, wait fifty-five minutes, and interpret the Cygnian's reply. Operating at 1/12 normal speed, the Cygnian didn't make for spirited dinner conversation. The Cask had been in the process of uploading a reply through its onboard AI when the breach occurred. Jollenbeck could find no record of the reply's content in the data fabric floating around him.

Again, he gathered the information and dumped the words into a convenient cache and dropped it to his side. As he reached to the Dump to probe further, he felt his chair skew sideways before righting itself. Metal screamed in painful remorse, and something snapped hollowly. The banging of metal against metal pierced the quiet. Light overwhelmed his optical sensors, like a brilliant burst of solar energy, which he'd not enjoyed in decades.

It was his brain that hurt, however. He engaged his Assist, having it call out, "Who's there?"

"It's Falco and Sister. Are you ready to go?"

"Go where?" Jollenbeck was still adapting to the brilliant light source beaming through the darkness, and he understood the ship hadn't powered up.

"Anywhere." That was Sister, although the Sanaa aspect, not Jollenbeck's favorite. The word was terse and to the point, with no semblance of compassion or warmth. It was what she was designed to be, a consummate problem solver. Jollenbeck recognized the benefits in the stronger personality, even if he preferred not to work with it.

"I'll follow. Are the lights out everywhere?"

"Yes, and you need wheels to conserve power." Falco held the light, and he knelt in front of Jollenbeck's high-tech chair. "Give Sister two minutes to attach them." Already, something whirred, and the chair vibrated.

"I have full magnetic lift on this world. The planet's field is massive. And power?" He laughed through the Assist. "I'm fully charged, and once the ship's back up, it'll provide what my Tesla can't."

"You won't have power, if that's what you're waiting on. Your magnetic lift is juice hungry, and we need you, Science Officer Jollenbeck. Lots of opportunities for new knowledge out there, and you might just be the one keeping us alive." Sister gave one last whir of her machine, shaking the chair, and she stood. "Magnetics off. You're rolling from this point on."

"Unless we hit a bump. We might let you float over that." Falco grasped Jollenbeck's shoulder and gave it a squeeze.

Sister growled, "Not on my watch."

Jollenbeck didn't see her expression, as Falco had him already on the way out the door, but he heard the tone of her voice. He'd like to see My Sister about now. He needed some explanations.

What did I miss in the Dump, he asked himself. This is Verboten, as far as I can tell. Nothing in the Dump so far indicates any differently.

He risked his LiDAR to see if he could locate any others aboard the ship. He cringed to think they were all dead. He hadn't had the chance to tell Franklin farewell.

That grieved him as the loss of no other crewman could.

—Chapter 4—

Dreadnaught *Vladimir Vladimirovich Putin*

General Arminius Agrippa
. . . demands answers that aren't so easily found

"WHERE ARE MY SOLDIERS?" General Agrippa ripped his question across the Uppernet as he left the Bridge, unworried who flashed and burned. Anyone who could access the Uppernet knew enough to be shielded, and if they weren't, what they got was their just deserts. The Army didn't coddle stupidity, and Agrippa didn't intend to start now.

That fool Tesfaye had tried to emasculate him before the crew on the Bridge. Agrippa wasn't a man to enjoy emasculation, and he had been fit to explode all over both Tesfaye and Devi. He would have too, except for the Construct that bound him to secrecy. Well, not exactly secrecy. This was no covert ops mission. His team of hardened and hardwired soldiers was fully funded by the

Wartime Cabinet, even if they were playing down the *Putin*'s script in this wing of the theater. Officially, the *Putin* was on recognizance, maybe one could say "support mission," out here to ensure things went the way they were supposed to go.

Agrippa chortled at that one. He would make sure things went the way they were supposed to go *if he could find his missing soldiers.*

Captain Devi with her pleased smile when she invited the crew back onto the Bridge, all those hangers-on! No way were twelve crew required on the Bridge. Gawkers, all! Agrippa could rip them apart with a single thought if he wished.

He wished, but he hadn't done it. There was a war on. A ship hadn't been available for his under-the-radar mission, and that meant sharing Devi's ship, and it was a good ship, fully equipped with the most modern Antigravity Repulsion Device, absolutely necessary if Verboten were, indeed, the destination his men had determined to be their best shot at achieving the mission's goal. Anything less than a top-level ARD, and that god-awful place would crumple their ship like a tinfoil toy boat and cast them aside like an unwanted bathtub bauble.

He flashed to Communications Officer Garian Ali, "Commo, you shunted up? I need your link nodules blinking *ASAP*. Just wrapped up a head-butt with Devi. The team needs to talk about Tesfaye and what has to happen. Briefing, stat."

Ali was Agrippa's IT Divo—divisional officer—and in command of Communications. *When* the *Roosevelt* was located—not *if*—he'd immerse himself in a water bath, plug into the comm console through his shunt, and rip through the wires hotter than even Agrippa. It was the reason for the water bath. The man was hardwired throughout his body, head to toe, although the water bath was only a necessary consideration during engagements and other heavy maneuvers. Having Ali aboard was a condition Agrippa had refused to budge on with Tesfaye, Devi, and all those pencil-pushing slagbrains back home. When the man plugged in, he *was* the ship, the brain of the beast, anyway. The part that ensured the victory that Agrippa demanded from this cursed war.

"Yah, here and shunting." Ali's image flashed over the Net with his words. Not so much a picture as a texture, a tone, a certain flavor of signal coming through the connection. Ali felt/tasted like filfel, with powdered peppers and crushed garlic. The man's Libyan ancestry, he liked to claim. Agrippa had other ideas. Ali harbored resentments over his people's long-ago treatment by the Italian usurpers who'd occupied his land and raped her for her resources. The powdered peppers and crushed garlic were his anger threatening to erupt. Good, Agrippa thought. As long as I can control it, the more anger the better.

"On my way," Agrippa pulsed, tight and so fast it was doubtful the *Putin* would recognize he had even sent it, that was if the vessel did happen to have Uppernet capabilities as refined as the Army's. He was certain it didn't.

As he walked, the meeting on the Bridge boiled over in Agrippa's head. Tesfaye's suggestion crawled under his skin, the man trying to oil the water, saying that they were on the right path, that "McAvoy, Hernandez, and Nissen are specially qualified, they have their orders, and their records are impeccable. Give them a chance to deal with the Envoy. They are aware of what's at stake, and they've been cleared by the highest power. Besides, they've been out of contact less than a day. Even keel, people. No need to rock the boat at this point in the journey."

Rock the boat. *Rock the boat!* This was war, and Tesfaye had boarded the *Putin* with Agrippa's team, on his side, he'd thought. His true nature, his *bias*, had started to show, thawing out of his ice-forged *bigotry* against the true nature of war, that of taking what was yours and crushing your opponent in the process.

Then Devi starting up with, "Now that that's settled, here's what we want to do," and that asinine blah, blah, blah voice of hers. He had no idea what she'd said at that point, and he didn't care. His eyes had seen red-tinged stars, and he'd wanted off that Bridge before he did something he might regret. He hadn't dared send to his team, even on the Uppernet. Tesfaye didn't have the state-of-the-art military communication upgrades his team had, but Agrippa didn't know what the man might catch short range. He couldn't afford the slip up. As soon as the *Putin* was designated as their ship of choice (or necessity, depending on how you wanted to look at the situation), Agrippa had assigned Combat Systems Officer Zilpah al-Din to harden Briefing—the old recreation area for the crew—with a shielded Undernet. The Undernet could be flooded with fake chatter. It wasn't foolproof, but since the Uppernet was classified and bespoke military, there wasn't much chance anyone would be looking for it, anyway. A second layer of protection was al-Din's secondary self, a cybernetic construct that lived in the physical walls and wires and systems of the ship. The CSO and her cybernetic counterpart merged each night, giving al-Din unfettered knowledge of whatever was going on in the ship.

Wouldn't Devi love to know that Agrippa's Combat Systems Officer was covertly prowling the Captain's ship even as she plotted against him! He wasn't telling. Not even Tesfaye knew. This was his team's little secret, hopefully providing him an advantage that would swing control of this ship—and all her military hardware—into his hands.

Agrippa passed numerous crew as he boiled his way through the corridors on the way to the old recreation area. The strips of recessed lighting overhead were no more than bands marking his passage down the corridor and offering flashes of his leathery face pulsing with irritation at Tesfaye's perceived failure to do his expected job. He strode up to the rec room door and paused, pulling his shoulders back and taking in a deep breath to swell out his chest. Mentally prepared, he pinged the door with a quick pulse of power, and it disappeared into the wall. He stepped through, his thoughts blank, giving the door a chance to completely close behind him.

As it did, Agrippa flashed, *"WHERE ARE MY SOLDIERS?"* leaving the ozone smell of lightning cutting across a night sky lingering on the Uppernet.

Every face in the room grimaced, except Commo Garian Ali. His shunt was plugged in at a comm console, his oversize hardware running through his body visible as outsized veins, with the link nodules at his joints flashing bright enough to be seen through his skin. Ali grinned. He'd known what was coming, and his good fortune was to be able to mute the General's anger through his shunt's connection.

Agrippa saw the grin, and he was satisfied. At least one of his team knew him well enough to understand what to expect. Get on board or get out of my way. If they wanted toast, they could eat it black. He wasn't buttering anyone's bread along the way.

CASK

—Chapter 5—

Interstellar Ranger *Franklin Delano Roosevelt*

Bishop Silvestre Zubizarreta
. . . whose heartfelt prayers draw some attention

"DEAR HOLY FATHER," I gasped, as I looked through the darkness, panting heavily, unable to quiet the flutters of total panic gripping my heart. This was a disaster of the most inopportune sort. The Envoy! How could this be happening? I pulled my cassock more closely around my neck, and outside my conscious volition, my lips once again set themselves into motion. "Dear Holy Father. Dear Holy Father."

"Are you injured, Your Worship?" The Acolyte, little more than a boy in his enveloping cassock, although plainer and pleated with far less folds than the Bishop's generous garments, grasped the Bishop's arm, offering a touch of the familiar in the nameless darkness.

"My soul, my emotions, every part of who I

am, yes, I am severely injured." Is the boy so cold as to feel no fear? Can he not sense the totality of our failure?

"I only mean, do you require medical attention?" By then, the youth was running his hands over the Bishop's arms, checking for obvious damage.

"The ship, are we truly at rest?" I pushed the invading hands roughly away. I had no bodily injuries, at least none that I could feel, although, when we regained the light, true eyesight might prove me otherwise. Still, I had spoken. Was the child so obtuse as to need physical proof that I could still walk, talk, and function as a man? Oh, to be saddled with an acolyte such as this one!

"Yes, Your Worship. Shall I endeavor to locate a light source?"

"Help me to stand, first." I took his hand when it brushed my forearm. I felt him stand, and with great effort—why does everything seem to always take such great effort!—I encouraged my cursed talisman of affliction to get me up in one quick launch. "Now, My Son, and do not waffle as you did before our Breaking of the Fast. With all your strength, pull, as though the devil is at your side."

"Yes, Your Worship. One, two—" His final word was obliterated by a groan of anguish from the Bishop as he rearranged his bulk and rocked his massive frame into the air.

"Does the gravity seem somewhat excessive to you, My Son?"

"If you wish it to be so." The Acolyte brushed at the Bishop's garments, creating a swish, swish sound in the darkness.

"I do not wish it to be so, and stop that!" Patience, Holy Father. Please give me patience. "A light, Child, for the darkness seems to invade my soul. Off with you!"

The boy's feet padded into the darkness, and the Bishop shook his head, glad for a moment of silence. He was saddled with a fool. Ah, for the comforts of his small cell in Rome. He should be so graced as to return there before his life was stolen from him on this godforsaken world. Yet, these were things he couldn't say, not aloud. To even admit to such feelings would heap shame upon him and his mission, and the Child would never find his way out of his navel and into the world of True Christendom and unlock the Unalterable and Holy Will of the Father.

"Child, Child, are you there?"

"I have light, Your Worship."

A glow brightened from the other room. It increased in strength as the Acolyte rounded a corner carrying a glowing globe in each hand. He pushed one off into the air the Bishop's direction, and it hovered at shoulder level for a moment, then settled closer to his knees.

"What is this, Child? Why does the Globe ride so low? I can barely see."

"The greater gravity offsets the internal compensators. Shall I attempt to make adjustments?" The Acolyte still held the second globe, causing the glow to illuminate his face inside his hood, giving him a hauntingly angelic appearance.

Truly he is but a child! I must speak gently. How else will he learn to properly assimilate himself into the Priesthood?

"It will suffice to light my way. Are there more Thracian Globes in your things? If so, perhaps some of our fellow passengers might appreciate our largesse."

"Only the two, Your Worship. I will be glad to share mine." The youth held it out with a subservient nod of his head, freezing in position as if waiting for the Bishop to speak.

"If necessary. For now, it's yours to illuminate your way. Are the doors operable?" *I suspect not, for they are powered. Still, battery backups? Surely the manufacturers of the ship would not wish passengers to be trapped in case of a power disruption. The settlements would be ruinous.*

"Manually, Your Excellency. It takes a firm hit with the shoulder. I will gladly loan you mine." The youth's face fought to contain a smile.

Amusing, he thinks he is! I will make him see amusing, as he is again laundering all our things, both clean and not, as a penance. Just you wait, Child. I will not be mocked.

Pounding sounds, like those of running feet, vibrated faintly through the ship, distracting the Bishop from his internal tirade. The large man reached to the wall and pressed against it gently.

"Child, are we to be rescued?"

"If you wish it to be so." Another nod of the head.

"Ooooh!" Yet, he controlled himself, turning his frustration to better use. "Oh, joy, I intended to say. Perhaps it's time to open our door."

The Acolyte had barely turned to look when something slammed noisily into the suite's main door. A second time and it swung open from one side as if hinged. First Mate Song leaned through the door, panting heavily, with a sheen of moisture on her forehead.

"Let me catch my breath." She held up one palm before leaning forward to put her hands on her knees, her back heaving as she gasped for air. After three deep draughts, she stood and hit the wall angrily with her fist, as if forced to say something she didn't want to speak aloud. "Are you ready to abandon ship?"

"Abandon ship?" The Bishop glanced at the Acolyte, then at their things strewn around the suite of rooms. They could not evacuate so quickly without time to pack, at least those items most important.

"Now, Bishop." Song seemed to just notice the glowing orbs. "You have Thracian Globes aboard? Those are your number one priority. Follow me." She slapped the wall again, this time differently, for emphasis, and she leaned into the corridor, calling, "Ssanyu! Have you located Jollenbeck?"

The reply was unintelligible.

"You two." She pointed with two fingers on one hand, first at the Bishop, then at the Acolyte. "Can you find the emergency exit?"

"Emergency? What emergency do we face? It's only a power interruption."

"Boy, you?" She looked just at the Acolyte.

"I believe so." The youth nodded, differently from earlier, but respectfully, just the same.

"I need to locate our Science Officer. I'll trust you two to make it out. If you need me, bang on the walls with anything heavy you can find. Someone will come, hopefully before the entire ship goes up in flames." She was gone as the final word rammed its message home.

"Flames, My Son?"

"What shall I gather first, Your Worship?"

The Bishop's mind was taxed to the limit. How could he pick and choose? There was the Holy Cross of the Crypt, his prayer books in seven languages, and the case of sacraments. They were blessed by the Holy Father. They absolutely could not be left behind. He felt he would swoon, as dizziness crept into his consciousness. Only by leaning against the wall could he continue to stand. As he regained his breath, he noticed the Acolyte's light was gone.

"Acolyte! Acolyte, where are you?" His heart throbbed. He was alone! He was alone! "Dear Holy Father. Dear Holy Father." He couldn't have stilled his lips if he'd tried.

The wisp of a boy appeared through a doorway, this time with the orb hovering at shoulder height. His face was shadowed by his cowl, but as he turned, it appeared he was removing a smile from his face.

"Child, have you not listened? We are to be evacuated! What shall we take?" The Bishop moved to a small table and picked up a ruby talisman attached to a silver cord. It was a remnant of the First Holy Cathedral, destroyed in the War for European Unity. It was sculpted from a remnant of the nave's rose window. It could never be replaced. Never! He slipped it over his head and tucked it inside his cassock.

"This way, Your Excellency." The Acolyte held an outstretched hand his direction. "I have collected our most precious documents in this case."

Yes, yes. I can see that now, a silver case, one from the small office I had claimed at the start of this journey. Yes, yes, the documents concerning the Envoy, the data chips, the encoded fund nodules, all of it. It cannot be left on the ship. All these things, much more important than mundane items such as clothes, or food, or ornament.

"I have my talisman, My Son. I believe I can find my trust in our God, as long as I wear it at my breast. Will you be so good as to take my hand? I feel somewhat unsteady on my feet today."

"If you wish it to be so." The Acolyte held out his arm. The attending orb shadowed his face, so that his expression couldn't be seen.

"I do wish it to be so." He smiled gratuitously at the youth. Perhaps he would one day master the skills of a servant, allowing him to be promoted to greater duties than a servant. God's will that it should be so.

"This way, Your Worship."

"My Son, I noticed your Globe. It's not at your feet." His trailed them, occasionally catching the heel of his sandal as he stepped forward.

"It's simple to adjust, Your Excellency. It takes but a moment."

He looked at the boy. He knew to do this? So easily? He had carried Thracian Globes to many worlds, and never once had he thought to learn to adjust their magnetic compensators. The boy's head was bowed respectfully, but his face was hidden by his hood as if laughing at the Bishop.

I will ignore his insolence for a time. We only have one set of clothing each, it now seems, and they will need washed nightly. Perhaps twice, as they will be in constant use. Let the child laugh then. I suspect he'll not find it funny when his hands are red and raw.

The Bishop began to wheeze with the effort to go so far and so quickly all in a very short time. The Acolyte paused, placed his arm under the Bishop's elbow, and together they made their way toward the exit.

—Chapter 6—

Dreadnaught *Vladimir Vladimirovich Putin*

Damage Control Assistant Indigo Popa
. . . who finds that a headache is the least of his worries

"WHERE ARE MY SOLDIERS?"

The words ripped through DCA Indigo Popa's head, leaving him with a searing pain in his skull. As Damage Control Assistant—nominally under First Engineer Manu Rodriguez, the Chief Officer of the Engineering Department aboard the *Putin*, but in reality, answerable directly to General Agrippa—he had been one of the first in the room. Training Officer Kasem Müller had been already present, standing at the back wall, his eyes taking in every person who entered. Popa had managed not to engage the man. Müller had been slated to be aboard the *Roosevelt* to ensure success with the Cask, then surprise! Hernandez had shown up on the roster, and Müller was with them.

CASK

How Popa wished it weren't so! As Training Officer, the man drove the team mercilessly, and Popa was certain there was something going on in the man's head that wasn't natural. His eyes—it was like there was someone else in there, the way he could flip like a switch, be a different person entirely, as quick as you could pulse a warning to the next man or woman to get out of his way. And the man never slept, never! Who could do that? Who? No one, that's who.

Popa kept his thoughts inside his head, most carefully kept every thought floating around inside his pounding head securely tamped away in a secluded quadrant of his brain that would never come to light. He was Damage Control. He didn't want to become the damage, and with Müller, who could tell when it might become your day?

Of course, Garian was there—Commo Ali over the lines—shunted in, probably even before Müller. He was a good man, had to be since he was the comm nexus for the team. He had to get along with everybody, even if he did sometimes have an acrid bite to his net messages. Still, the Commo was easy-smeasy with everyone, whether officially or just shooting off their mouths in private time.

That was how you stayed private, shooting off your mouth. Anything through the links, and anyone had access if they tried hard enough.

While Popa was trying to stay under Müller's

radar, Auxiliaries Officer Blythe Rossi slipped in, the only one of the team naturally aspirated, with her only concession to upgrades being her Transdermal Communication Device. Technically, she ran all the stuff that wasn't Weapons or Engine Room, neither of which the Army had access to unless the ship engaged in wartime maneuvers, which meant Rossi was currently the least encumbered member of the team. They all knew, however, the reason she was aboard.

Control.

Rossi was under constant biometric monitoring as a control factor to determine how the rest of them were performing, er, holding up to the unusual situation of being on board a vessel skippered by a captain who was an outside and mostly unknown factor. Rossi must know they could do it, as she had limited access also, but it hadn't slowed down her amorous streak, which was tracked religiously by several voyeurs on the team.

Half of CSO al-Din was present. The cybernetic portion of the Combat Systems Officer—the cyborg her—was probably off searching for secrets about Captain Devi to twist her authority until General Agrippa got everything he wanted.

Weapons Officer Finola de Jong didn't show, but with al-Din in attendance, that was moot, as de Jong reported directly to al-Din. She probably had a hyper-wire plugged into her eye, courting the ship's weapons' systems so they would be friends when the time came.

Operations Officer Ellery Martin was the last one in. A narrow man with a thick shock of tight hair, he had a slippery feel to him. Something going on below the waterline, a tricky dick, so to speak. Popa was still trying to work it out.

Not present? Popa didn't expect Tesfaye, nominally theirs but out of Agrippa's loop; Naval Flight Officer Jelena Sharipov—on loan to the Army for this mission—with her transdermal receptors for contactless flight control; or Kaua'i Mori, Pilot-in-Command, even superseding the General during war maneuvers, although Mori had the right, Popa ceded, having survived an attack on the *John Fitzgerald Kennedy* when the Cygnians first appeared out of the dark depths of the distant Cosmos. Even Captain Devi was willing to listen when Mori stepped onto the Bridge, just that now was not the time for someone they weren't sure was on their side. This meeting was not for them, although another three to dissipate the General's wrath wouldn't be unappreciated.

Popa felt Ops Martin shoot something through the Net to Auxo Rossi. He looked from Martin's face to Rossi, to catch her smile before she glanced away with a red flush creeping up her neck. With Commo Ali shunted in, Popa could slide along the fiberlines to eavesdrop on Rossi's bios. He slipped in, acknowledging Ali on the way, a short blip of electricity out of courtesy, and noted Rossi's elevated heartbeat and rising temperature. Popa grinned. He didn't have to know what Martin sent—couldn't, without some difficulty, because it was a direct message—but the biometrics said it all.

The team—those interested, anyway—would get a peep show tonight, if they could get Ali to shunt in for the duration.

Popa caught Müller's eye, then the man looked to Martin, then to Rossi, his flat eyes skipping like stones on water. Something like sweet sauerkraut filled the invisible lines that stretched across the room—Müller's unmistakable angry aroma—and Ali's shoulders drooped.

"Sorry, Indy." Powdered peppers, and the link to the bioscan broke.

Gads, can Müller read my thoughts? Popa considered the idea and brushed it aside. Müller might be a monster, with so many personalities that he would be clinically insane by any rational standards, but no one could read minds. That's what the Net was for.

Agrippa ended all extraneous chatter, calling, with tempered moderation, "de Jong, anyone? al-Din, she's yours."

"Working with my Construct, ser. de Jong's

getting me past the firing sequence firewall. Everything you say here, she'll know."

"Okay, then. We've got a Mission Commander that's not on our side, not the way I need him to be." He released a Dump of what had taken place on the Bridge, the part between him, Devi, and Tesfaye. It arrived hot and angry, and several people winced. Agrippa's face didn't shift expressions, other than to bore his eyes into Müller, who looked impassively back at him. The conversation was on the Uppernet, and the air was thick with the transmissions. "We've got three missing men, all of them on the *Roosevelt*. How can we assure they're doing or have done their job?"

A muscle twitched on al-Din's face, and she lifted one finger.

"Speak up, Combat Systems Officer. What do we not know?" The General's leather face tightened around his mouth almost as if he had wanted to say more but had stopped himself.

"I've verified with Commo that we don't have access to the full ship's systems. That's outside our negotiated parameters and will likely restrict our chances for success if and when we need to act once the *Roosevelt* is located. Ask our DeCA" — how his title sounded when spoken aloud— "to let out his inner side. He can run the probabilities faster than any computer aboard this vessel."

"Officer Popa? What can you tell us?"

Seamlessly, Damage Control Assistant Indigo Popa released control of his body and felt himself float off to the side, watching, waiting. He would return, but the when would be up to his secondary personality. Genetically engineered from Eastern European male stock, there were two Popas inside the normally self-effacing charmer: the first was Indigo, who felt relaxed around most people; and Merlyn, a computer-fast thinking machine that could draw down his bodily reserves at a heart-stopping rate, if required, to achieve phenomenal results in record time.

The DCA cocked his head and began to rapidly speak aloud, with tongue clicks indicating divisions between ideas, concepts, or individual items.

//Merlyn present * click * how are you doing, General * click * I've been listening in and think I can offer insight into the situation * click * how would you like me to proceed * click//

"WHERE ARE MY MISSING SOLDIERS?"

That burned across the lines quite well. Even the DCA's eyes narrowed at the jolt ... and in Merlyn mode, he was hardly connected to the Net at all.

CASK

—Chapter 7—

Interstellar Ranger *Franklin Delano Roosevelt*

Captain Vicente Falco

. . . finds frustration in an increasingly desperate situation

"ENGINEER SSANYU, hold up a moment. Wheels aren't getting Jollenbeck out of this craft, not with that blockage just ahead."

"We are making good time, sir." Sister maneuvered Jollenbeck's chair around a mound of fallen debris.

Despite Sister's determination otherwise, it wasn't going to happen. The corridor was only slightly canted, suggesting a quick passage out, and allowing us to make good time, yet the twisted superstructure piercing the ceiling just ahead of us suggested differently.

I shook my head. We needed good time. I was catching whiffs of smoke. The passive fire suppressants should kick in—I was surprised they hadn't already—and I wanted off this craft before they did.

I had to know whether to forge ahead to find a way through the obstruction, or if we needed to plan an alternate route. Our limited lighting wasn't reaching the other side.

I knelt before the Science Officer's chair. "Jollenbeck, is your LiDAR online?"

"And functioning perfectly." The Assist across his chest oscillated in cascades of undulating sine waves, at times tightly spaced or drawn out, reflecting words spoken and inflection. Moods could be read through the images on the Assist, as well, once one was familiar with interpreting the various colors. A hint of yellow infused the crest of each wave.

I couldn't help chuckling. I read an impatient snort in the words. In the colors of his sine waves, to be precise. As if my Science Officer were rolling his eyes, telling me, "Naturally, it works. Do I look broken?"

"Excellent. We want to be offloaded before the fire suppressants kick in, if at all possible. How bad is the damage just ahead?" I didn't move out of his way. There was no need. I would be just another blip on his sensors, a glowing image of a man amid the different objects his LiDAR would ping, plot on a coordinate graph, and build into 3-D objects intelligible to the human brain. Holding still was my best option.

"I have three alternate routes mapped." That came from Sister.

Her eyes were on me, and I could catch her corneal implants shifting through the data stores the Engineer carried with her at all times. Normally the data schematics couldn't be seen in her eyes, but the light was low, and with her face shadowed, the false corneas gave off a blue glow, with the darkened lines of the alternate routes banded in darker shades. It was hypnotic. We'd had a late-night conversation or two—My Sister and I, any-way—and I'd been captivated, unable to take my eyes from hers.

Whew! I pulled myself away from that, breaking contact with her eyes. I stood and moved beside the Science Officer's chair. "Aldrik, your assessment?"

"The hull limits my visibility." It would, being all metal. LiDAR wasn't magic, just good science. "Where it's damaged, I can see through to the other side. This corridor ends just past this obstruction. I don't recommend further attempts this way. The level above this one is clear for a section but appears blocked by the same debris we see ahead. The corridor below has not been penetrated. And Captain?"

"Yes?" I glanced down. The Assist glowed green with laughter. I wasn't sure I was going to like this.

"Sister's eyes are beautiful, I agree."

Yeah, it was laughter I'd seen. If I could get to the man's shoulder, I'd punch him so hard he'd be laughing to the other side of the moon, that is, if this planet had any. I didn't remember.

"Just saying, Captain. No offense." Still glowing with laughter.

"None taken." I wasn't offended, just irritated that the man could read me that well. It was probably all that LiDAR technology. Maybe I needed some of that. As a distraction, I called, "Sister, pick us a route."

"Two of the paths lead directly to an outside access hatch and give us a ninety-four and ninety-seven percent margin of success, consecutively. I suggest the third. However, the margin of success drops to sixty-seven percent."

"Your reasoning is?" I had a couple late-night conversations still on tap with a few of my favorite people. I didn't like sixty-seven percent. I was growing more partial to ninety-seven the longer we stood there.

"We've yet to locate Medical Officer Franklin. I judge the risk of losing him is worth a detour to the Medical Bay. He will be with the Cask to ensure the safety of the Envoy."

"You're always so right. What's the plan?" I didn't have to like her assessment to agree with it.

Does that make me a good captain? I like to think so.

"We can create an access panel in the floor and drop to the lower level. The food stores will allow us to access the Medical Bay, if we disengage the refrigerant lines and cut through the back wall. It abuts the surgery facilities."

"Create an access panel. In the floor." I looked up and down the corridor for seams. "You mean, by hand."

Over our heads, the smell of smoke had turned to a greasy haze. Soon it would begin to fill the lower sections of the corridor. I was perfectly willing to use my hands to scrape away the floor, creating an access panel, if that's what it took.

It seemed that's exactly what Sister suggested. Together, we worked a metal strut free from the damage ahead of us, and I tapped it against the floor until I found a seam. I slammed the end into it until I could wedge it in as a pry bar. I try to stay fit, but I was sweating buckets by the time I had the panel freed. Sister accessed her diagrams, indicating the various wires, tubes, and infrastructure I could safely destroy, and eventually, we reached the ceiling below. It simply lifted out of the way, and I set it aside.

"Science Officer Jollenbeck, you first." I motioned him over.

"May I engage my magnetics?" Yeah, his

Assist was laughing at me. The man knew me better than I knew myself.

"I'd rather you roll in and take your chances. You want to run your batteries down, I'm good with that." I watched Sister, wondering what comeback she'd find for that. Something dry and absolutely correct, I suspected.

"Wait, Aldrik." There was concern in her words, and she dipped her head and turned away. She flashed her light through the new opening.

"My Sister, is that you?" I suspected so.

"Yes, Captain Falco. I suggest this path may very well end in disaster, if we continue. If the Envoy lives, Medical Officer Franklin will do his utmost to ensure its survival. Ship's Android has been able to initiate contact with me by draining all residual capacitor power from the drives. She was fully connected in the Nexus when the anomaly occurred and is still attempting to disconnect with as little damage as possible. Guests Ghost, Recon, and Pyro are already outside the ship."

My Sister looked up, and I noticed her eyes. Information surged across them too rapidly for me to make out.

"Can Android get the soldiers back inside to remove the Cask? Have her tell them it's for Franklin. They won't agree, otherwise." The three men seemed quite capable at their jobs. They should be, being career Army officers. It was plain they didn't care for the Envoy. Several times I'd seen them looking at it with pure hatred in their eyes. You'd think the Envoy dedicating a portion of its life to the peacekeeping endeavors between Earth and the Cygnus cluster would be a good thing. I didn't quite trust our Army guests, although they'd done nothing to imperil the mission up to this point.

"I'll ask." Her head was bowed again, and she spoke very softly, making her answers hard to hear. The ship had begun to creak ominously, and dread painted my armpits wet.

"Sixty-seven or ninety-seven. Decision time is here."

"The doctor is, indeed, with the Envoy. Our Church guests are being escorted from the ship by First Mate Song, and Android has been forced to relinquish further contact. We are on our own, Captain."

My Sister lifted her head, an expression of irritation crossed her face, and I knew Sanaa was back.

"We're going for ninety-seven percent, Ssanyu. Does that still take us down this hole?" I shined my light downward. The corridor below looked like yesterday, before there was a crash. When my ship was whole, and I could fly between the stars.

"If I may, I'll lead. There may be damage the

LiDAR is unable to sense." Without waiting, Sister dropped into the blackness and disappeared. Her light flashed upward, and she called, "Jollenbeck, are you coming? We're clear down here, but I don't know how long that will last. Pull up your shorts, and let's get this caravan moving."

"Get your caravan moving, Science Officer." I grinned and kicked one of his new wheels with my foot.

"Yes, sir. Step back, if you don't mind." The Assist blinked his words at me, the image blue with trust and sincerity.

I did. His chair made a clicking sound, then hummed as it rose into the air. He moved over the newly formed hatch, and with more precision than I'd ever be able to muster, dropped smoothly into the hole.

Flickering red from among the rubble followed me as I dropped through after him. Jollenbeck was back on his wheels—due to Sister's insistence, I suspected—and she motioned towards the way we'd come on the upper level. I raised my eye-brows.

"Are you sure?" I wanted her to be very sure.

"Ninety-seven percent." She almost smiled, and I caught it.

The walls of the ship vibrated, and a faint hissing noise turned into a crescendo of rushing air.

"Fire suppressors initiated. Move, people!" I

wrapped my hands around one side of Jollenbeck's chair, and Sister had the other. We leaped forward at a run. The sound of rushing air was from inside the walls. Without ship's sensors and the mainframe to correlate the sections of the ship aflame with the necessary suppressant jets to douse the fire, the entire system would trigger to ensure the destruction was minimized. In a worst-case scenario, the corridors would also be flooded. If we were in them, that wasn't a good thing.

"Left!" Sister yelled the word, and immediately, we veered that direction, Jollenbeck's chair turning the corner easily. I wondered at that, but as I was running top out, it wasn't my prime priority. Being able to breathe something besides suppressant foam was.

At the exit hatch, I held my palm over the access panel, hoping to the Bishop's god that the Android hadn't stripped the capacitor reserves from the hatch's release mechanism. The door was spring-loaded and would swing free of its own accord. The latch was powered. The access panel glowed, but dimly.

"Sir, if you please." Jollenbeck's Assist spoke to me as the words arced across the screen. "My batteries are not depleted just yet."

His chair rose when I backed away, and I remembered the corner. No wonder we'd made such good time. He'd been helping. He extended a manipulator from the arm of his chair, touched an access point on the control, and said, "Now, sir."

I slapped my hand on the panel, and the door released with a screech of unoiled metal and lifted out of our way. Outside was a lush, green world, more like Earth than I remembered Earth being like.

"Are they serious? This can't be Verboten. Verboten's a wasteland."

"Not in my book. Let's go, Jollenbeck. Follow me." Sister stepped to the door and motioned for him to follow. So, she'd known he was using his magnetic lift all along.

I'm the Captain. I should know these things, and I can't if people don't tell me. Hear that, people? I'm the Captain, and this is my ship.

I had to say that before I stepped outside. Well, think it. Once I looked at the vessel from the outside, I might very well wish it was yesterday, and that it stayed that way for the rest of my life.

The crescendo of air from earlier became a timpani rumble, and turning, I saw yellow foam filling the corridor behind me and rushing to greet me at a presto pace.

"Yikes," I yelled, and I leaped into the arms of the Verboten canopy, hit a branch, skewed sideways, tumbled several times, and landed directly on my rump on a large limb.

I reached for Sister's hand to help me stand, but

CASK

I was irritated at my Science Officer. His Assist glowed bright green, and I don't like being laughed at, even by a crewman as brilliant as Jollenbeck always tries to convince everyone he is.

My backside was sore, however, so I had to put Jollenbeck aside. I'd deal with him later. Now, I was happy to be able to stand, if barely. Even that hurt almost more than I can say.

Then the limb gave way, and we tumbled down the hillside.

—Chapter 8—

Dreadnaught *Vladimir Vladimirovich Putin*

Second Mate Ulric Jónsdóttir
. . . in which a fresh face gets his attention

"I HAVE SOME TIME." Second Mate Operations Officer Ulric Jónsdóttir settled comfortably into a chair across from Third Mate Flight Officer Signy Melnik. "Second watchshift isn't until sixteen hundred. But then you know that, so I guess you're trying to blow me off?"

Melnik, as Third Mate, would be covering the third watchshift, and she yawned broadly. Neither officer had been on the Bridge during the earlier flareup between the Captain and their visiting Mission Commander. If Melnik had been there— or even privy to the details—she would have been staunchly in Captain Devi's corner. She felt an overwhelming admiration for the woman, although she dared anyone to call it an emotional attachment. In any case, the Captain's achievements could never undo the shading of her skin or the sultry color of her eyes, so there was little chance of an attachment (daresay a liaison), even were that possible aboard ship.

"Short morning, long night." Melnik pushed her sleepiness away and tucked her clipped, dark hair beneath her cap. "We should eat. Get what you want, but I'll take something thick, juicy, and bleeding. You can talk while I'm filling up."

"It's vat grown, you do know that." Jónsdóttir recalled about a dozen conversations along those lines. All the food aboard was produced from the same nutrient stock, though he allowed that most of the fresh vegetables were likely from Hydroponics. He stood, his uniform falling easily around his stick-thin frame, and he ducked his head of white hair under a sign that pointed to the exit. It wasn't especially low, but he was especially tall, and he naturally ducked at things overhead.

"Will it bleed?" She already had out a personal glass from her pocket, and she shifted images as she spoke.

"It will for you." Jónsdóttir let himself smile, and as he turned away, he felt it erupt into a laugh.

"Enough, Officer," Melnik barked.

Jónsdóttir glanced back to see her smiling, and he chuckled as he moved toward where he could see food steaming in the warmers. Melnik and he made a good pair, as a working marriage, anyway.

As for more, he was always on the prowl for a hookup, but Melnik put more emphasis on being an officer than a woman, and besides, Jónsdóttir was pretty certain she had her eye on the Captain. He didn't know that it would ever go anywhere, but it certainly dampened his enthusiasm for pursuing Melnik's private company for anything other than an occasional late-night chaser after her watch.

He nodded at several people and noted Technician Anouk Mohamed in Environmental Control and Life Support sitting with someone he had yet to meet. He pressed his lips together hard to redden them, to make them pop against his ice-pale skin, and walked to the table next to them and made a point to speak to Second Helmsman Ceasar Papadopoulos, as if that was where he had been headed all along.

"Hey, Assistant Pilot, where's your main man?" Azizi Quispe, he meant. Of course, Quispe thought his relationship with Papadopoulos was packaged, tied up, and neatly set on a shelf when he was away from his quarters, but no one could miss the stars in Papadopoulos' eyes when Quispe walked into the room—and his disappointment when Quispe treated him as another crewmember, one subordinate to him (although that's exactly how it was). Jónsdóttir knew the pain of unrequited love, even if it was normally momentary on his end, and he felt an empathic rapport with the thick-necked and heavy-featured helmsman.

"Off doing shipboard things. On the Bridge, if you care to know, but it doesn't matter. He wouldn't pay me mind, anyway." Papadopoulos' eyes tossed with storm. "You, Jónsdóttir. You and Melnik. Anything?" He grinned wickedly and twisted his fingers suggestively.

"Your dreams are bigger than my abilities, my friend. You continue to believe in Quipse. He'll come around someday, and if not, at least you have his nights." Jónsdóttir clapped him on one shoulder and turned to move away when the Second Helmsman grabbed the hand in both of his.

"You are a good friend to me, Ulric. Thank you, and good luck with Melnik. Someday, the gods will smile on you." He grinned and pushed Jónsdóttir's hand away.

Jónsdóttir winked at him. He wouldn't share the reason he knew better. That was up to Melnik. If she wanted the ship to know, it was her news to share. Of course, she'd have to admit it to herself, first, and Jónsdóttir wasn't sure that was happening anytime soon. He turned to Technician Mohamed as if surprised to find her in the Mess.

"Anouk, they let you out of the cooling system?" He smiled in teasing. Anouk was heavily tattooed, with thick legs and thicker, wiry hair. She was the self-proclaimed God of Weather aboard the *Putin* and made sure people knew. She liked to laugh, the more inappropriate the subject matter, the better.

"And you, Ulric, they let you out of Cargo? Maybe they figured you, Thin Arms, might break if a pallet shifted during maneuvers." She threw her head back and laughed, deeply and vigorously, with her eyes closed. Finished, she motioned to her companion. "My friend, Jelena. Jelena, this is my friend Ulric. He looks as if the wind will blow him away. Thank Isis there is no wind aboard the *Vladimir Putin*." She let out another laugh, not quite as raucous or lengthy as the first.

"Flight Officer Jelena Sharipov?" Jónsdóttir was interested. She was the backseat mission commander, arrived with the Army team they carried on board, although she was a Navy squid. That seemed a shame, but it wasn't likely she had a choice in her assignment. He looked at her hands. She was reputed to have transdermal receptor matter injected directly under the skin on her palms, enabling her to plug in remotely to the ship's computers during maneuvers. It was rumored that each of the special mission team was armored—if that was the word—with technology the rest of the crew could only dream about.

"Word's gotten around, huh?" Sharipov smiled, showing a wide set of bright teeth. "I've heard of you, also, Officer Jónsdóttir. By the way, what's with your name? I thought Jónsdóttir meant

John's Daughter. Is there something I'm missing under that uniform of yours?"

"Or something *Ulric* is missing!" Mohamed guffawed, holding her stomach as she wrapped a big hand around Jónsdóttir's arm, completely encircling it.

"If you want to see, sometime . . ." Jónsdóttir smiled. He was used to the teasing, and he wasn't bothered. It sometimes made a good introduction to an even better night. He reached out a hand to Sharipov. "M'lady, if I may?"

She offered hers, and he took it, working his long fingers across her skin, making sure to massage her palms gently but thoroughly. It felt like skin, and he was vaguely disappointed. He guessed he'd hoped for clips and nodules and wires and leads—the things you might find in any hardware device.

He air-kissed it, something he'd found women liked, and he released it, saying, "I'm getting food for my partner. She's waiting. I'm sure we'll meet again, Flight Officer Sharipov, that is unless you mean to avoid me."

She laughed. "It's a ship. Not likely I can do that."

Jónsdóttir felt ten kilos lighter as he walked away, as though he might float if he didn't keep his thoughts on the ground. Then something wet hit him on the back of one ear. He turned to see Third

Mate Melnik with a straw to her lips, and she signed the letters for food in the air.

Yikes, Jónsdóttir thought. He'd forgotten the meat. So alive it bleeds. He grimaced and picked up his pace towards the steaming food.

CASK

Interstellar Ranger *Franklin Delano Roosevelt*

Medical Officer Richard Franklin
. . . in which something heavy gets even heavier

"NOW, THAT'S NOT a landing I want to repeat. Do you hear that, Boss?" I didn't know if Falco was receiving. If he wasn't, I'd have to make a point to repeat it. "Note to Med-Tab, save comment for future reference. Remind me when I next see Captain Falco."

A few moments earlier I'd been divided, half in the Holo-Lab with Jollenbeck, and half loosely immersed in *The Three Sirens of the Cascades*. Looking around, I found myself on the floor surrounded by jumbled medical supplies.

The *Sirens* was much more appealing. And where was the power? Everything was shut down. I couldn't even sense the movement of air. On a ship, air is always moving. Always.

At least it wasn't total darkness in the Medical

Bay. The Cask glowed with an internal light of its own. It was, by nature of being a self-contained environment, self-powered, with full internal diagnostics and backups. I hadn't reviewed the battery half-life on the machine, but then, no one had expected ship's power to conk out.

I pulled myself to my feet, checking my limbs for damage, glad to find myself reasonably pristine. Internal film packaging from a medicinal vial clung to my sleeve. I pulled it away, surprised when it popped with static electricity. It was not supposed to do that. The static dampers must be offline. Definitely not good.

I tapped the Med-Tab at my throat with my index finger. "Ask Toofer to evaluate the dampers. I'm getting static buildup in the Medical Bay." Get Sanaa on it, and she'd wag the dog before she let it go.

An orange light blinked on the Cask in a series of three quick flashes and two slow ones. It repeated itself. I'd not seen that signal before, but I knew immediately what it meant. An upload interruption. The Stranger had been in the process of communication with someone on the ship, and it had been interrupted.

I pulled a dedicated glass from a waist-high counter and stroked it on. It was self-powered. I turned it, shifting the display to landscape mode, and tapped the Envoy icon. An image of the creature—I had no other word to describe the strange being inside the Cask—filled half my display. The image was from Hanook, the Cygnian's home world orbiting the star Kepler in the Cygnus constellation. The creature had heavily lined skin, although I knew from our conversations that it was relatively young, not having yet mated or sired offspring. I imagined it to be the Hindu elephant deity Ganesh, except with fewer arms and less jewelry. Funny, the Envoy referred to itself as Cygnian rather than Hanookish, although I didn't see anything in it. Our references were learned ones that had meaning only to Humanity. The Cygnian used the words we assigned, and I'm sure one was as pleasing as another.

I tapped the glass to see what it had to say.

—Medical Officer Franklin, I have been perusing the ship's information feeds, and I notice we're coming to a planetary body. By my calculations, we will be within visual range within one of your hours. Will we be landing on this world? As this is my first trip through interstellar space, I am very interested in observing other worlds besides my own. May I request access to the ship's external video feeds? If so . . . there, something unusual. I am picking up a message from a small satellite calling itself Space Buoy 571. How unusual. I am not hooked to any exterior information feeds. Yet, the message is coming through quite clearly. Notice, Notice. Magnetic Tides Prevalent. Proceed With . . . no, no! Power spike! Must withdraw. Must withdraw—

Ah, Stranger. If only you could communicate with us in real time. I tapped the download icon and spoke, "Envoy, we seem to have landed, possibly on the planet Verboten. I trust you are uninjured. The Cask seems to be fully operational. Ship's power is off, and you are currently operating on internal batteries. Be cautious with your power use until we get the ship back online. I'll be waiting on your reply."

The message turned into a virtual tornado and was gone, sent to the Cask to be integrated into the Envoy's awareness. To the Envoy, the conversation would feel as if it were in real time, although it most certainly wasn't. I had fifty-five minutes before the glass would receive a reply.

Odd, something acrid was in the air. I drew in a deep breath and coughed. Smoke. I could see it in the glow of the glass. I pushed the Envoy's icon away and probed the glass for any live feeds from the ship, hoping to discover more information. Every source was marked with a red "X" indicating . . . what? Power plant offline? Internal code violation? Guest rebellion? I had seen the friction between the Envoy and the Army, but it hadn't escalated beyond pointed comments, and the Envoy was insulated from those, unless the three soldiers had begun surreptitious messages I was unaware of. Would the Envoy share that with me? I had no idea, but I hoped so.

The Medical Bay door thumped, and loudly, startling me, and I fumbled the glass, sending it out of my hands and against the corner of a cart that had rolled from its position across the room. With a sharp crack, it flashed dull blue and went clear just before it impacted the floor.

The door thumped again, and it flew open, rather than sliding sideways as it normally did. I was unsure whether to exclaim in dismay over the damaged glass, or to reprimand the people who had startled me, causing me to drop and damage it. There was no opportunity to link another glass to the Cask. Until the ship came back online, there was no other way to communicate with the Envoy.

"Medical Officer Franklin, we are here to assist you."

I forced my eyes to the door to find the Army representatives entering. Pyro was fully through, in full uniform, with weapons and munitions attached all over his body. A light bored from his helmet, illuminating what he happened to be looking at. An internal green glow filled the inside of his helmet, giving his face an eerie, otherworldly cast. He carried a large power rifle in one arm, lifted halfway as if prepared to fire.

He probably was, as were the two men who

followed him in, Ghost and Recon. Ghost's face was illuminated in red, and Recon's in blue. For identification, I'd been told during one of our chats.

I brought myself to my senses immediately. If these men had been sent to help me—I certainly hadn't called them—then I assumed the ship was in some sort of mortal danger, meaning the Envoy was in danger. That changed everything.

"Thank you, Loki." My name for the green-faced man. He accepted it, as did the other two, whom I'd given personal names of their own. It was my way, and crew and guests seemed to enjoy the familial interaction from the ship's Medical Officer. "Is the Envoy in danger?"

I noticed the way his face hardened; and he glanced at the Cask and away again. Buster—Ghost—and Search—Recon—did the same. As long as they performed, that was all I asked. They could have their opinions so long as they didn't act upon them.

"The ship is in danger. Everyone is evacuating." Pyro nodded at me. "This way, if you will, Doctor."

"Let me get your help with the Envoy. Officers, if you will?" Without the magnetic lift—and I dared not use it and run the batteries down—the Cask and its occupant weighed in at nearly half a ton.

Ghost let out a deep breath and looked away.

Recon's jaw tensed, but he kept his eyes on me and didn't say anything.

I had turned Loki's question back on him, asking very politely and with a smile. These were good men. I didn't doubt their character. I also didn't doubt they would assist me with the Cask.

"Men?" Pyro jerked his head. "The good doctor is asking for our help. Let's move."

The three officers hiked their weapons over their shoulders, working their straps to hold them securely, and without a word spoken between them, began to ready the Cask for transport. Pyro made his way to each corner, hitting the catches with his fist to release the bulky balloon wheels, which hissed as they aired themselves up. Ghost began readying to disengage the power and information feeds, to shunt the useless cables aside, and seal the access ports. Recon stepped to the window, glared into the glow emanating from the transparent sheeting, before releasing the grab handles at each end of the Cask.

Whew, I thought. I'm glad they're Army. I don't know any other branch of the military that could hate an alien race so strongly, and still provide the Envoy the help that might save the creature's life.

I did notice one thing. Neither Ghost nor Pyro looked inside the Cask. Not one time. Only Recon. I'd seen the look he'd given the Envoy. I didn't know which I preferred.

I did know this. If the ship was evacuating, I wanted to get moving. I let out a sigh of relief when Pyro called out, "Ready to disengage and roll! Ghost, anytime. Doc, you follow, and we'll get you out alive."

Alive? It was that bad? My stomach churned as I lifted my personal glass from a counter, slipped it into my belt, and prepared to follow them out the door.

CASK

—Chapter 10—

Dreadnaught *Vladimir Vladimirovich Putin*

Pilot-in-Command Kaua'i Mori
. . . who is surprised to find something to do

"I KNOW MY PLACE." Pilot-in-Command Kaua'i Mori strode down the *seventh* corridor, up the *fifth* set of steps, and avoided the *fourth* lift he passed by. It wasn't like he needed to *get* anywhere, because, as he'd been told so abruptly by both Mission Commander Tesfaye and his *lovely* second-in-command Sharipov, there was nothing for him to *do,* so he might as well get comfortable, enjoy the journey, and wait for them to call him to the Bridge.

Who, he'd wanted to ask, had been on the *J.F.K.* during the initial Cygnian incursion? *Who*, pray tell, had the intuitive foresight to order Weapons to go hot even before the first Cygnian vessel had fully translated into Jovian space? *Who*, and they really needed to think about this, *who* had survived that battle, despite the full-on and total loss of the *J.F.K.* and all other hands on board? Not Tesfaye. Not Sharipov, he had wanted to say, but he hadn't. Mori was a soldier, a rule-follower, a man who recognized that there's a reason for military hierarchy. In the heat of battle, a superior can't lead without the confidence that every decision made under overwhelming pressure can be backed up with an order that will get done without question.

When he was guiding this vessel, that's what he'd expect from the Captain and the Commander. Even Sharipov would have to jump when he said jump.

Not now, though. He didn't even have a section of the ship he could call home. Neither did Tesfaye or Sharipov, as the three of them weren't part of General Agrippa's "team," but that was beside the point. He was the one suffering. Mori. The man who would make a difference when this ship ran across a Cygnian vessel, and they would, they could bet their latest space torps on it. The Cygnians were everywhere and *snea*-ky. The truth was, as Mori saw it, they were so different from mankind, they barely acknowledged our existence. They hadn't even known Sol System was claimed by Humanity, thought we were plants, or something like that. Just because we don't grow *pseudopods* . . .

CASK

Mori let his inner tirade fall silent, scattered all along what now amounted to far more than seven corridors, because he was at his quarters.

His and three others from the *Putin*. After all, the Commander couldn't deign to bunk with a lowly lieutenant, and Sharipov, well, female, and enough said on that. And the moon grit on the inductor was that the three of his roomies had been displaced by the General's team, and they weren't making the distinction between them and him.

Mori took a deep breath, already mentally exhausted, straightened his uniform—he needed to change into his greens now that the Commander was through with him—and pressed his hand to the plate beside the door.

As the door slipped aside, the fresh aroma of spruce forests and high meadows surrounded him, and Mori felt his heart slow, his blood cool, and his frustration settle into a churning undercurrent he felt he could safely ignore for a time. From beyond his vision, soft laughter accompanied the clattering of wood pieces, and it sounded like one tumbled to the floor.

"Careful, Cousin. That you, Kai?" The voice was Korhonen's—sorry, Ziggy's—and a chair scraped the floor. A head with fair hair and green eyes peered down the entrance hallway, then said, "Oh, it's you. Come on in. Soren and I are playing Mölkky. You are welcome to join in. Though, you may watch if you don't wish to play."

"Mölkky?" Mori began undoing the buttons on his jacket, and he stepped around the corner. "Hello, Soren. I hope I'm not disturbing."

"Yes, you are, very much disturbing." A solid man with thinning sandy hair, Soren Hansen was arranging twelve numbered pins on the table, and he took the final one that had fallen to the floor from Korhonen and separated two to add it to the middle. "Any man who comes aboard our ship and takes over our recreation area and forces us to change our quarters from there to here is a man who disturbs everything—"

"I've told you guys, I'm not them. I'm not on that team. I don't even get to hang out with them—" Mori involuntarily gesticulated with one arm, and he felt his blood churn. His anxiety skyrocketed before he could take a deep breath to calm himself. And he had to sleep in the same room with them!

"Hold on, Pilot." Korhonen interrupted and wrapped a big hand around Mori's wrist. He chuckled before giving his cousin a stern look. "Soren's just being a bull in a china shop, like always. We feel you got off on the wrong foot with us, and we're sorry. It took us some time to understand how you intruders—no offense intended—are interlinked."

"Not very." Mori let out a tired sigh, as deflated as he had been incensed, and about as quickly.

Besides, his leg was warning him it needed to be recharged. He could probably go another two or three days—a week in a pinch—if he didn't have to run or navigate especially uneven ground, like stairs, which meant using the lifts, which he was avoiding. "Not at all, truth be told. They just told me I had nothing to do until we meet the Cygnians, if we ever do. I'm just Lieutenant Pilot-in-Command, and as this is you guys' ship, I'm a loose cannon. I can be a table leg, and no one would care."

"Sort of are, aren't you?" Korhonen grinned at his cousin before looking back to Mori, to see his expression fall. "C'mon, Lieutenant Pilot, we know about the leg. Take a joke. It's just us three. Relax." He leaned towards the bronze-skinned man and rapped his knuckle sharply on Mori's leg, giving off a resounding thunk before Mori could react or protest.

Mori glanced at where the man had connected with his leg, and he grinned as he looked up. "You mean it? I can hang with you guys?" He slipped his jacket off and tossed it to land on his bottom bunk so near to folded it hardly made a difference. The bottom bunk had been one concession he'd received, of the many he'd requested. His leg, he'd insisted. There would be times he could hardly climb up top.

"If you will learn our game." Soren rapped the

table in a firm manner, with his mouth firmly set. Then he broke into a grin. "Watch for a time. You may like it. It's a favorite of my homeland."

"My homeland, Cousin. Don't forget there is a border between our two lands." Korhonen leaned forward enough to cuff Soren on the shoulder, being careful not to disturb the numbered pins.

"Finland, Norway, who can tell which is which? The trees grow the same height on both sides of the border. You, Lieutenant, you will join us?"

"Kaua'i. Thank you. Do you mind if I plug in my leg? It has to charge for several hours, overnight if possible."

"Please. Every night you do this, charge the leg? I have not noticed."

"Not usually. I've been taking lots of stairs, and the steps drain the batteries." Mori had his belt undone, and he dropped his trousers, folded them, and landed them on the bed as neatly as the jacket. Under his shirttails, and beneath his loose white drawers, one leg was oiled bronze skin, finished out in dark hair to match his head, and the other shimmered in a titanium alloy. Exposed hinges and servo motors, flush to the surface, were traced with thin ribbons of light that glowed brighter when Mori moved that part of his leg. The center of the alloy thigh held a touch pad for logging in and out and inputting instructions. There were several slots for plugging in outside devices.

"The ship's lifts won't work for you?" Soren frowned. Everyone wasn't permitted on all portions of the ship, but the lifts generally accessed the whole vessel.

"It's the leg. They create interference. Sometimes I stumble when I come out. Near as I can tell, the leg's computer has to reset to reengage the balance and stability programs." Mori had the leg powered down and undid two attachment levers at either side. Then he twisted hard, hopped back, and leaned the leg against the wall. Two metal studs protruded through his skin, and he used his hand to snap them flush with the bottom of his stump. Using the titanium leg for balance, he opened the top, pulled out a short cord, and ran it to an outlet on the wall. The leg beeped once, a countdown readout appeared on the touch pad, and it began counting from six hours.

"Here." Soren shifted a lightweight chair Mori's direction, and Mori eased himself down. "That's from the *J.F.K.*?"

"And this," Mori, said, tapping his head through his thick bush of hair, giving off a similar thunk to the one from his leg.

"Do you plug that in, also, my friend?" Soren chuckled.

"Nah." Mori was feeling comfortable, and he didn't mind telling part of his story. "When the

Cygnians took out our ship, they nearly got me. That's the reason for the leg," he nodded at Soren, "and this holds half my brain in. Titanium alloy, courtesy of the Army." He tapped his head again.

"A man we can respect." Korhonen pronounced it as if it were now an accepted fact that couldn't be denied. "You do know my title is Data Technician."

"And mine is Information Technician. I manage the computer systems on board the Putin," Soren chimed in.

"Between us, I'm sure we can reprogram your leg and eliminate the interference with the lifts."

"Seriously? You guys, that's great. Please. You'll have my eternal gratitude." Mori thought, *No more steps!* How had he doubted these guys? He hoped Technician Kumar turned out to be as great. His bunk was always a mess, but the man, maybe he would become a friend, also.

"For a man such as you, a man we can now respect for his bravery in battle, we are glad to help. One thing only, you must learn our game. Here, take this ball . . ."

And the game was on.

CASK

—Chapter 11—

Interstellar Ranger *Franklin Delano Roosevelt*

Android
. . . in which many parts become one

[[BURN! BURN! Must withdraw! Disconnect! Disconnect!]]

Android had its body differentiated into twelve fully extendable arms stretching tenuously from a central nucleus outward, emulating quite closely the spiders from Earth recorded in its databanks. However, unlike the small arachnids originating on Humanity's home world, this spider would soon resemble a human, that was, if each of its appendages could be disengaged before the trauma invading the entire ship consumed it.

It felt it was being eaten alive.

Android nominally maintained a default self-awareness as a human male, unless he was required to take on female form, or morph into a shape that reflected neither gender. Then she identified with femininity and charm, or took on a neutral stance, unlike the precision and self-control he pulsed with as a male.

At this juncture, caught in the electrons blasting his nerve centers with information, he needed his male attributes, and he claimed his internal human aspect vengefully.

Twelve arms remained physically attached to the inanimate structure of the *Roosevelt*, drawing data from the three Nexus datapoints feeding through each link. The ship vibrated, shivering with impending doom, but Android was unable to disengage. Instead, information fed into him, burning, burning, filling him up with what he didn't want to know.

[[Heat, heat, feeding through ship's lines; must break connections; damage will be catastrophic.]]

[[Cask online, uploading! Disconnect! No time to initiate communication protocol; disconnect immediately!]]

Android sent a surge of commands through all three datalink points carrying the kilojoules of transfer energy to and from the Cask's energy links. If even one should remain open when the coming power surge swept through the Medical Bay portion of the *Roosevelt*, the processors in the Cask would sizzle and burn.

[[Must not burn! Disconnect!]]

First came external power. A twist of a charged

capacitor, and it was done. The Envoy's power uplink was severed. Android couldn't physically disconnect the power leads, but he could sever the ability to send energy along those leads. He double-checked the level of charge in the Cask's battery banks, relieved to find them full, even as he was aware he could do nothing about it if they weren't.

Severing the communications link would leave the Envoy in virtual isolation. Android was regretful to do so without explanation, but nanoseconds were the difference in life and death. Time for explanations would come later.

If everyone still lived.

Android barely had time to register autonomous data that still surged into the Cask's communication centers. The link was severed, so he dismissed it as a random anomaly. He didn't have the two nanoseconds to spare in working out the discrepancy. He had the third datalink to sever, and there were still eleven additional connections throughout the ship to extricate. Even one nanosecond was too long to worry about the inconsequential.

Before withdrawing his first arm, Android took advantage of the unexplained signal and piggy-backed the mysterious data, forcing in an encoded Data Dump—hopefully apprising the Envoy of the current status of all crew and guests on board—and sent his last signal to the Cask.

[[Bleed Envoy protocols to Storage Port 2, mark!]]

The information also surged into the Secured Internal Nexus inside Android's central core, his "thorax," awaiting retrieval if something should happen to the Envoy. It was an emergency backup package, entrusted to the Android, if something just like this should occur. No one had expected it to be put into play, but then, no one had expected the *Roosevelt* to be compromised, either.

Android's arm physically jerked from the Nexus connection, and he contracted the appendage, absorbing it into his central core. He felt the returning matter flow into him, filling him up, like a glass of cold water on a hot day.

Or, better stated, like a hot infusion of coffee on a cold, cold morning, running down his throat, and warming him inside where he was chilled the most.

Android touched the data nodes of the crew, noting their latest recorded locations and activities: Falco on the bridge, along with Song, both in full control of their local situation, and he severed their connections, withdrawing his arms. Franklin had been—was!—in Holo-Lab in situ with Jollenbeck, trapped in a repeating Holo-loop as the energy surge swelling through the ship discombobulated the ship's normal functioning capability.

CASK

[[Sever connection!]]

Android felt the fractured energy feed as the Medical Officer collapsed back into himself and Jollenbeck unraveled his Holo-link, ending up back in his quarters. Dimly, he felt Jollenbeck's frustration at his failed results going unrecorded as his world went black around him.

[[Ssanyu, prepare for Data Dump.]] If it worked. The engineer's signal was fluctuating, indicating her section of the ship was receiving the worst of the power surges. Android found the Army soldiers running down a corridor toward an exit, and the Bishop and his acolyte exiting their quarters. He prepared the Dump, giving everyone's current position and possible safe egress points, and he sent it along Ssanyu's datapoint connection.

[[Grab it, Engineer. I'm severing contact.]] And he let her go, pulling in two more of his arms and letting them fill him up with their completeness. He hoped the Dump surfed the surges and made it to her.

The engine strained, and through the datalink, it felt it was about to overload. Android reached into its core to adjust the load on each of its output boards, only to be burned severely. He triggered shutdowns across the breadth of his engine datalink. The vessel shuddered, then the sounds through that datalink faded into an eerie silence. The arm snapped out, withdrawing rapidly into his body. He tried to connect with the Bridge when he was scorched by heat. It was already aflame, and he snapped the datalink and freed himself from yet another datapoint.

[[Six nanoseconds! Death now imminent! External sensors! Life support! Everything failing!]]

In an act of desperation, wishing to maintain personal continuance, and now assured all physical persons on board the *Roosevelt* were accounted for, Android prepared for a full fire-suppression implementation, when the lights flashed on around him. Through his datalinks, he felt the ship come alive. A request hit him from Ssanyu, directing him to send the Army team to the Medical Bay to aid Franklin with the Cask. He paused the nanosecond it took to comply, threw two Data Dumps over the Intraship communications datapoint to Ssanyu and Jollenbeck before the ship went dark, and his data-points began to burn.

[[Hot! Hot! Withdraw! Withdraw!]]

Android broke all connections. The violence of the reflex reaction spun him around and threw him to the floor, as eight remaining arms flew his direction in one giant rush. Absorbing so many so quickly overtaxed his body's pain-dampening abilities, and he screamed out in torment as the material swelled into him, changing his shape and form from a twelve-legged spider to something more resembling a man.

Gasping for air—he did breathe, both as a venting mechanism and a way of sensing the quality of the local atmosphere—he pulled himself to his feet, and he hit the ground running.

[[Fire suppression! Delay engaged? Everyone must be out before it engages.]]

The same went for Android. He might not need air to breathe, but he wasn't made of torches and M-wire, able to extricate himself from corridors filled with fire-suppressant foam.

[[Run faster! Must run faster!]]

And that's exactly what he did, hoping he'd engaged the delay sequence, his legs lifting higher and higher, his feet pounding the floor.

—Chapter 12—

Dreadnaught *Vladimir Vladimirovich Putin*

Training Officer Kasem Müller
. . . who discovers someone else looking through his eyes

TRAINING OFFICER Kasem Müller unplugged himself, and he stepped away from the charging and maintenance alcove nestled in one corner of his quarters. He (if he could be said to be a he) had requested the specialized equipment to be shipped aboard as personal gear, and over the first few nights, he had assembled it while the rest of the team spent their REMs in individual bunks or paired up with another soldier, whichever was their proclivity of choice.

Traino Müller? No such weakness. He didn't sleep, or rather, he didn't take downtime, except for his required hour at lunch. Everyone else disappeared to the DFAC there-or-about the same time, so it had been decided to make that the slot for his personal refueling.

Nominally (as far as the team was concerned), Müller spent that hour boning up on the latest Cygnian engagements, in quantum contact with Earth, and reviewing personnel files and qualification assessments. He declined visiting the Dining Facility and never, ever ate with the team.

It was funny to the FusionTech Laboratory back home that Müller's time in his personal dining facility was the only time the Training Officer *wasn't* in quantum contact with Earth, a tongue-in-cheek prod that was a laugh at the team's expense.

It was also funny to them that there was no such man as Training Officer Kasem Müller. Rather, there were three men who made up Training Officer Müller in four-hour shifts, hinting at the reason Indigo Popa (and a few others on the team) were perplexed by Müller's sudden shifts in mood and personality.

As a precaution, Müller was designed with a safety protocol to operate for short stints in autonomous mode. You never knew what might come up when your operators were light years away and only human—very good, and very experienced, but very human. Müller could give standard responses, make light conversation using short phrases—as well as learn to predict appropriate responses to new situations based on previous experience, even when not overseen by an operator. Yet not even FusionTech's top-level drones could process fast enough to engage in high-speed interactions with humans with any believability. Hence, the Müller drone was staffed 23/7, every day, using three drivers in four-hour shifts. This afternoon, Operator One was suited up, fully encased in a powered Exosuit, with full-vision goggles strapped to his face and resting on his forehead. An aide was plugging in leads that trailed across the floor to a massive mainframe across the room. Operator One was running late. He hadn't been able to get fully comfortable in his suit, and since he was at the beginning of a four-hour stint, comfort was paramount. While he got his plugs in order, Müller was temporarily in autonomous mode, which was okay, as he was still in his quarters, standing quietly—Operator One trusted with reasonable certainty—and waiting to turn over control to his driver.

Of course, Traino Müller didn't know (or care) who his driver would be. He didn't care about anything much, not if his drivers didn't care. The assignment for the operators was originally to be a brief stint of a week, max. Get on board the *Roosevelt*, make sure the Army team took care of the Envoy, and if they failed, they had the warhead in Müller's head to finish the assignment aboard the *F.D.R.* if necessary. Of course, no one hoped it would be necessary, but in times of war, small evils to combat greater evils were the name of the game. After Müller was assigned to the *F.D.R.*, with everything set, the technicians at FusionTech, being incredibly *German,* had demanded such rigorous perfection with the tech integration that the Müller drone hadn't received final approval, and Captain Xavier Hernandez had stepped up to take his place aboard the *F.D.R.* The Müller drone was already in place and functioning as a real person at the War Office (Field trials, field trials, and more field trials to prove that it could be done!), and he couldn't be shut down. It had been weeks before boarding the *Putin,* all the while maintaining a viable persona for the veritable Traino, and they were about full up with it. Driving the robotic drone had become routine and monotonously boring.

And that was the reason the operators were using Müller to liven things up on the *Putin.*

Operator One lay back on his SenseCouch. The Couch was one of three, comprised of half a meter of IntelliFoam, designed to compress and expand with his motions when his Exosuit was powered up. A predictive AI operated the IntelliFoam in the Couch, keeping track of which operator was driving Müller, and on which Couch, to ease the trial of four hours of constant activity in a robotic drone body connected via quantum entanglement from dozens of light years away. Once Operator

One was in position, the sides on the Couch lifted, forming a low wall around him so he didn't inadvertently tumble off during more active periods, and he raised a thumb. The aide returned the hand signal as the Operator lowered his goggles to obscure his vision, and he pressed a large green button labeled *Operator One*. A few feet down, the two other Couches boasted green switches for Operator Two and Operator Three. No lag at switchover was allowed. The change must be smooth and invisible to those on the *Putin*.

Operator One let his eyes roam the view through his goggles, only sensing the deep purple glow of a pending connection. The color seemed to stretch into infinity. He had no eyes, yet, not in the Müller body, anyway. His arms were still his, sensing the firm, slightly heated pressure of his Exosuit, and his legs still resting on the SenseCouch, the padding pressing gently against the back of his thighs and calves. Then the world shifted with a subtle jolt, and Müller's quarters on the *Putin* came online, slightly fuzzy at the outside edges before clearing up completely. Operator One felt the fabric of Müller's uniform on the back of his legs, the cool air blowing from the vent in the wall, and heard the subtle hum of the ship's engines that was so faint that normal people would probably only notice its absence. He noted he was standing, his usual default position after unplugging from the maintenance alcove.

Operator One strode to the door with quick and sure steps, totally confident in his control of the Müller drone, and he pressed a palm that was as warm as a human one, and even slightly damp, against the sense pad. No one, even if they were yelled at by Müller, would know the difference from a human. Müller's breath would be warm, moist, and carry a slight odor of mint, possibly a supposed previous meal, or occasionally the fetid odor of an upset stomach.

The hand on the sense pad? Calculated genius. The drone could easily ping the door and trigger it to open, but a hand is only human. What further proof would anyone need? Any *robot* could ping a door. An unmodified human would have to palm it.

And Müller had to be as human as they came.

The door slipped aside with a whoosh, and Müller stepped outside and pivoted to look down the corridor, his feet firmly planted a half meter apart. He locked his hands behind him, one set of meaty fingers encircling the wrist of the other. He waited quietly, although there was no activity anywhere that he could see, just the soft glow of the overhead lighting and closed doors opening off to additional rooms consisting of personnel quarters, storage areas, and sundry other rooms.

A door down the corridor whooshed, and the

light from inside fell into the corridor. Müller called, even before he could see anyone, in a loud, crisp bark, "de Jong, snap to."

Weapons Officer Finola de Jong appeared through the doorway, a green duffel over her shoulder, and she turned to see who had spoken. When she caught sight of Müller, she jerked erect and attempted to salute, only to be too encumbered with the duffel for success. She cleared her throat, sloughed off the duffel to let it fall to the floor, and pressed her hand to her left breast.

"Sir."

Müller returned her salute and fought a smile as she dropped her arm.

"Headed somewhere, de Jong?" Müller had his hands locked behind his back again.

"Sir, I didn't see you there. Yes. Laundry. What can I do for you?"

"Didn't see you at Briefing today. Busy?" Operator One was using Müller to harass the Weps officer. She was on the record for being plugged into the ship during that hour, and no one could question her absence, but she wouldn't know that he knew that.

"Sir, my apologies. In Weapons. I was plugged in. You can check the log if you want. I've nothing to hide."

"Is that so, de Jong? I'll tell you what. I would like a team training session at fourteen hundred hours. Everyone possible, you especially. I've been reviewing qualifications records, and it seems there are some things we need to fine tune." Müller hadn't changed position. He lifted his chin slightly, raised his eyebrows, and narrowed his eyes. The Weps officer paled, and he knew his expression had done the trick.

"Anything wrong, sir?" de Jong glanced at her duffel.

"That duffel bothering you, de Jong?" Back at FusionTech, Operator One chuckled. He knew she was jittery, but he wasn't finished, yet.

"Laundry, sir. I scheduled a slot at half-thirteen. It's been tough getting in with the extra bodies on board." She took a deep breath but didn't let her gaze drop a second time.

"It looks like it's about to get a little tougher making that appointment. You've got a team to round up. Briefing at fourteen hundred. Acknowledged?"

"Certainly, sir. Briefing at fourteen hundred. Thank you, sir." de Jong broke her position, grasped the duffel's strap, and tossed it back into her quarters. She took another deep breath, moved toward Müller, and when he didn't step out of her way, turned sideways and slipped past, barely avoiding his shoulder.

Müller allowed himself a chuckle when she was gone. He was an electronic machine, totally connected to every public feed on the ship, and a few that weren't. He tracked de Jong's movements as she stepped into the lift, her respiration elevated and her temperature pinging off the charts.

Today was going to be a good day, a very good day. Well, the next four hours, anyway. What Operator Two got up to was his business, but for four hours, Operator One intended to have fun.

CASK

Interstellar Ranger *Franklin Delano Roosevelt*

First Mate Jiang Song
. . . adds interest with a counter melody

"PEAS PORRIDGE HOT, peas porridge pot cold. Peas porridge in the pot nine days old."

I don't know why that old rhyme reverberated in my head as I ran down the dark and decimated corridor. I suppose it was the Bishop. I kept imagining him eating spoonful after spoonful of porridge, while the kid was starving. Of course, I'd never seen the Bishop eat; the kid, either; I had to trust I'd done right by sending them off on their own. Jollenbeck deserved my attention, and now. With power down, he was going nowhere real fast. I knew how much power LiDAR stole from the system. Magnetic lifting and thrust? Cough up your insides, cause you're giving up everything to go there. Maybe we'd get lucky, and the Tesla would be up and operational. No promises, no trust. It was up to me to be the Science Officer's backup plan.

Peas porridge hot ... I wished for a larger glowstick. The one strapped to my wrist barely lighted my footsteps, but I couldn't take time to search for another. Nearing the Science Lab, I found the bulkhead cracked. I first saw it on the wall as a deep shadow that made no sense, then the floor canted, and I understood. Which end of the ship was falling away? It depended on whether we'd landed level or not. Not, was my guess.

In the tangle of darkness and the twisting fingers of shadows, I let my thoughts run. A bad thing, but it was what I did. I stopped and looked around me, unsure where I was. I forced myself to think. I'd been on the Bridge, which had been aflame. Down three levels to encourage the fat man and his small one to leave their religious paraphernalia behind, even as I was convinced they'd refuse. The Thracian Globes, however, that'd been brilliant. I wished they'd had a dozen more. I traced my steps in my mind, held my light to a sign on the wall, and smiled. If the lift was operational, I was where I needed to be. It wasn't, but I knew where the emergency stairs were, and I climbed over sparking debris to the door I knew to be around the corner.

It was canted in its frame. I kicked at it with the flat of my foot, my strongest hit only moving it a centimeter or two. Again, and again. Peas porridge cold . . . ran through my head. The fifth or sixth kick—I'd lost count—and the metal shrieked as it scraped against the floor. I glowed, renewed with energy. Once more it shrieked, I pressed against the gap, and I was through. A red emergency light on the wall blinked on, holding for a second, before flickering and going dark. It blinked again, repeating the pattern. Stairwells should have self-powered backup lighting. This looked to be no more than a capacitor releasing a charge. I had no idea what could steal power from the stairwell lighting. I let it go, as I was to the next level by then. This door was twisted, its top hinge pulled free, and I managed to clamber over.

"Jolley?" The Science Lab was directly across, and the door was wide. I threw myself inside, calling, "Officer Jollenbeck? Are you in here?" If he was in his quarters when this hit, he was toast. He wouldn't be, however. It wasn't like him. He loved his lab, and that's where he spent his time, nights, even, when the Captain let him.

Something caught my foot on the floor, and I knelt to see what it was. Packaging. I aimed my glowstick at it, reading, "Full Range Wheels, 60 cm, 4-Pk." To the side was a power drill with a driver attachment. I laughed. Someone had been by. My guess, the Captain and the Engineer. I shined my glowstick along the floor, and sure enough, wheeled tracks meandered out the door, the proof seen in the thin layer of debris covering everything.

Before I thought, I keyed the comm panel to check in, to see if anyone else was on board, surprised there was no response. Puzzled, I looked to see the display blank. Oh, I'm a fool, I thought, laughing. The light was dimmer, and I shook my glowstick, disturbed the batteries were giving out. It should be good for twenty hours or more, even under maximum brightness. I touched the lens, and my finger came away blackened. I realized it had grown smoky. There had been the fire on the Bridge, but the ship's fire suppression system would have contained and damped that.

If ship's power was totally functional.

I remembered the stairwell light. I sniffed, finding an acrid, burned plastic smell in the air. Peas porridge in the pot nine days old ... An epiphany put wings to my feet, and I fled the Lab, working on ways out of the ship. When the suppression systems blew, they would fire all over the ship, all at once. The rumble started under my feet, at first no more than that. I heard it in the walls, even as smoke began to clog the air. I kept my wits about me, refused to think of Captain Falco and our late-night talks after the rest of the ship had quieted for lights' out, or of Medical Officer Franklin. Number 2. He called me Number 2 in a way that made my heart warm at his words.

CASK

I pushed away whether Science Officer Jollenbeck had made it out. His insight made him invaluable. He had to be saved. And Engineer Ssanyu. Saving her was saving two. The Army and religious passengers, and the Envoy, I wished them godspeed, but it was my crew that would break my heart and slow me down if I thought too long on them. All I could do was aim for an exit and hope there was nothing occluding the way.

I leaped over broken wall panels, dodged dangling conduits, and found a lift door, forced by someone, with no lift inside. Just below was an exit, if I could get there. The air pressure increased, and I knew the yellow foam was already filling the corridors. I would be dead if I didn't move now. I leaped into the empty shaft, landing hard at the bottom. The wind was knocked from me, and my arm hit the side of the shaft, killing my glowstick. Yet, there was light. The lift doors were slightly parted, and a glow from the corridor suffused the empty shaft with just enough illumination to spur me to action. I forced the doors apart, turned right, and found the outside world, green and bright, calling to me. I didn't hesitate. With every fiber of my being, I tore up the floor; and as I determined to tell the story when I was reunited with the rest of the crew, the rushing air displaced by the building wall of foam punched me out the door, flinging me into the unknown.

—Chapter 14—

Dreadnaught *Vladimir Vladimirovich Putin*

Captain Kalinda Devi
. . . who uncorks a Russian doll

A BATTLE RAGED in Captain Kalinda Devi's chest.

It might be more accurate to say it raged in the Captain's mind, her head, her thoughts, intentions, or even in her determination.

Yet, she felt it in her chest, in her thrumming heart, that fist of muscle that kept her aware of how much control she must exhibit as the master of her ship.

Devi sat in her chair, one hand resting lightly on a bank of controls built into the arm, and the other at her waist. Her feet were pulled slightly under the front edge of the seat, and the tips of her shined shoes just rested against the floor. She looked around the Bridge, outwardly calm, breathing evenly, evenly, evenly as she kneaded the slightly nubby texture of her prayer cloth. She had obtained the fragment in the Trikuta hills, in the cave temple of Mata Vaishnodevi, in Mother India, herself. It was as though the spirituality and vibrancy she had felt during her visit to the sacred and holy place lingered with her each time she stroked the remnant of her time there.

This day, this very day, she struggled to regain the calm the cloth normally brought to her. Instead, the distaste of General Agrippa's virulent verbal fisticuffs had her reserves of calm shredded like the claws of the Bengal tiger upon which the revered deity Maa Durga surveyed the battlefield. She was the goddess of war, but also a protective mother goddess, and Devi held the goddess' mother image in her mind. As the mother goddess, she would release her wrath against the wicked, and Devi was certain General Agrippa fell firmly into that despicable lot.

Even so, even so. Devi might be the master of her ship, but Agrippa, as hateful as the thought was to her, was the reason for this voyage. And Tesfaye. What to be done about Tesfaye? As Mission Commander, he had nominal control of her bridge, but she intended she would cede nothing else to him. She had one demand of him, the same she had voiced before accepting this mission, although accepting was not the word that told of the true events of the past weeks. Conscripted. Yes, they conscripted her ship for what she had begun to expect was less than a peaceful purpose.

Her demand? Control. She expected Tesfaye to be the master of General Agrippa, to hold him in line, and she was now afraid she had taken on board a *fattu*, a cowardly person.

"Ma'am?" First Mate August Murphy, with his wide, muscular shoulders, had moved to her side.

"Mr. Murphy." Devi was relieved her voice sounded calm, and she tucked the small prayer cloth into her sleeve without noticing she had done so.

"When you are ready, Captain. No rush, no hurry, just letting you know I'm available."

"Yes, right." Devi stood, shifting forward to slip off the front of the seat and onto her feet in a flawlessly smooth motion. She tugged the hem of her jacket without noticing her action, and she turned slightly to face Murphy. "Is there any additional news of our visitors?"

Murphy raised his eyebrows in a question.

"Come, Mr. Murphy. I am aware of the goings-on aboard my ship. What has your ops team uncovered?"

"About the General." The copious freckles visible on his forearms seemed to burn brighter with his response.

"You have another recognizance sweep in action?" She could almost smile at that. It was a reason the man was her First Mate. He had the initiative to step up and do things without explicit instructions.

"No, ma'am. Well, yes, but you aren't asking about those."

"No." She noticed Helmsman Quispe glance her direction, but he turned back to his screen when he saw she was speaking with Murphy. As well. She would make time for Quispe later.

"They have hardened the old recreation area with an Undernet."

"An Undernet? We can't filter out the chatter?"

"Shielded, ma'am." He clenched his jaw, revealing his frustration.

"Ah. That would be al-Din. I am led to believe the Combat Systems Officer is quite talented, and I suppose her strengths have not been understated. A second self, I believe?" She pursed her lips as if she wanted confirmation.

"A cybernetic construct, yes. It was, um, unavoidable."

"As was this mission." Devi was thinking about Tesfaye and her insistence that he control Agrippa. *Fattu*, although she would not say that aloud. "Here's what we want to do: If we cannot read through their Undernet chatter, we will have to find another way."

"I have a few ideas, ma'am."

"I thought you might. You have the Bridge,

sir."

"I have the Bridge, ma'am."

The Captain moved smoothly past the Executive Officer, giving the muscular man plenty of space, and toward the lift. She caught light chatter from the stations on the Bridge, heard the click of keyboard inputs, and a chair creaked as someone stood. She didn't look to see. The Bridge was no longer hers, not for a time, anyway.

The doors of the lift closed behind her with a pneumatic whoosh before she turned. She hadn't wanted to glimpse the Bridge. She was too invested, and there were times she needed to remember herself and make for herself a place of inner peace. She closed her eyes for thirty seconds before opening them and sighing deeply. That was all the inner peace she had time to claim. She touched her comm and spoke with assurance.

"Helmsman Papadopoulos, this is the Captain."

If his line was clear, he would respond promptly. If not, her comm would give the familiar double ding, and she could post a message, although he would respond if she simply disconnected. As the Captain, she expected no less.

"Papadopoulos. Yes, Captain?" Behind his words was the bright sound of conversation in a large space.

"You are where, Helmsman? I would guess the Mess." There was no "schedule" for the chow hall,

CASK

as the ship was large, and assignments dictated that crew worked around the clock. The DFAC was open twenty-four/seven, and if the cooks weren't on duty, there was food prepared, either cold or in the warmers, and everyone bussed their own tables. It was the middle of the night for some crew, just as for others it was lunchtime.

"Yes, sir." He didn't say anything else, waiting on her.

"Who's with you?"

"At my table, Captain? No one. If you need me to step out of the Mess—"

"Around you, Helmsman. At the other tables. List, please." Very focused. She had intended to request a meeting to talk with him about her lead pilot, but that wasn't for now. This was more important.

"Jónsdóttir was just here. He was asking about Quipse—"

"Just names, Ceasar. Only those present." Clear your thoughts, Helmsman. Focus.

"Okay, then. Jónsdóttir, eating with Melnik, I think, though she was across the room. Then, um, yes, Anouk Mohamed, you know, from Engineering."

"I know the technician. Names, Helmsman. Anyone else?"

"Certainly, lots. Oh, one of the visiting military team was with Mohamed." It sounded like he sat up and grinned, his words infused with excitement.

"And that was?" Devi waited, patient for a moment, but not for much longer.

"Russian, perhaps? The one with the things under her skin."

"Sharipov?" Devi widened her eyes in anticipation. This might well suggest an opportunity for her First Mate to investigate.

"Sure. That's her." Papadopoulos chuckled. "Jelena. She and Jónsdóttir seemed to hit it off."

"Is Sharipov still there?"

"Mohamed is showing her the ship. Sorry, sir."

"Interesting. Thank you, Helmsman." The woman surely did not have the General's confidences, not if she was touring the ship with the Environmental Engineer, as Devi knew Agrippa had called a meeting immediately after their confrontation on the Bridge.

Devi disconnected as the doors to the lift opened. She was sure Murphy would want this news. Perhaps the woman might be a way to break into Agrippa's tightly locked-up team.

She stepped into the corridor, the bands of lights stretching in front of her, no longer thinking of the lift doors as they whooshed closed behind her.

CASK

—Chapter 15—

Interdicted Colony World *Verboten*

Engineer Sanaa Nakato Ssanyu
. . . in which one becomes two becomes one

"AAAA-AH!" THE TREE hit hard against my back, the prickly bark pressing into my skin. Even as I cringed, I took comfort in my part in ensuring Science Officer Jollenbeck yet another day of life. Captain Falco was a man of action, which I appreciated more than he knew.

The tree, however, I appreciated less. My fall from the ship was into a ravine, and I had tumbled several times. I was unsure if the Science Officer was powered at the time of our exit. If not, his chances for survival were very low. I couldn't bear to think of it, and I let my consciousness subside, the surface of my awareness churning like hot oil, popping in bubbles of coherent sentient strings, my thoughts erupting into the barrier of reality, slamming into the feeble meat that forms our brains, and demanding attention, all at once, and all the time. It was tiring, and I called as I released control to my beloved twin, "My Sister! Strive for aggression!"

Saana slipped beneath the wave of consciousness as she tumbled from the ship, struggling to orient herself. As she fell, the world faded, blurred, as in a fog, slipping by, My Sister sponging away the pain of her impact with the tree. My Sister could do that, take her thoughts from her, controlling their body when she desired. Thank God she desired it seldom, that she found serenity of mind in release, in the dreams of submission, rather than in the energy of life. Without Saana, My Sister would be all caring and softness, and nothing would get done.

Yet, for this one moment, Saana was grateful for My Sister's thoughtfulness, her willingness to be her cushion against the world, to accept what she could not absorb, and to make her life bearable. My Sister had taken the brunt of the impact from the tree, and Saana murmured her appreciation, before assuming control once more.

Saana blinked twice, fast, to pull up information from the ship. Within her vision, overlaid on all that was before her, her eyes revealed what she didn't want to know. Reset. Reset. The words blinked green, then faded. New, red words appeared. Reset Failed. Reinitiating Now . . .

CASK

Saana double blinked again. Ship was certainly dead. There was other information she could access . . . the Cask, perhaps, if it survived . . . Jollenbeck's chair, possibly. Personal comms, when within range. Personal biometrics, recorded conversations, even videos recorded within her wetware capacitors. She needed the ship, though. She needed to know what had happened.

"Engineer Ssanyu, injuries, report." Captain Falco knelt at her side. His uniform was torn along one leg, and there were bloodstains on the fabric.

"Nothing I can't handle. Jollenbeck needs us." Her back hurt when she leaned forward, however, and she stifled a groan, forcing herself to stand. She was grateful for the Captain's hand at her elbow. Whether he knew she hurt more than she let on or it was simply courtesy, she didn't know. Her vision faded for a moment, and she heard My Sister say softly, "Thank you, Captain. I'm fine now."

"My Sister?" He frowned.

"Only for a moment." Control returned, and she took it, looking around, searching. "Science Officer Jollenbeck," she called loudly.

"Sanaa," and Falco took my arm, pointing through the foliage, first left, then right.

"Captain—" She saw it, the ship, a small portion, anyway. It was worse than she could have believed. The outer hull was peeled away just where they'd exited. There was no telling how badly the rest of the ship was damaged. If she were to extrapolate from what she could see, and from what had been revealed inside, the damage was catastrophic. They were far down the hill and had no way of climbing upward to learn more. If someone was there, they were beyond reach.

"Look just there, Engineer." Falco pointed beyond the canopy of dense greenery, away from the ship. Saana pushed a hanging branch of thick leaves aside. Plant life abounded far into the distance, and a small city lay nestled in the crook of a river.

"St. Petersburg?"

"That's my guess. It's the only city on Verboten. It's where we were headed, when . . . this happened."

Saana watched him carefully as he glanced up the hillside, his face telling what his words couldn't say. His life had been ripped from him, along with his ship, his crew—many of them close friends— and the lives of his passengers.

"Captain! Sister! Is anyone else with you?" The voice called, twisting as it filtered through the dense growth, and they searched. Under the canopy was all shadows, occluded protuberances of twisted vines and leaves, with few patches clear enough to see any distance.

"Up! I'm here." The voice called again, and they looked higher. There was Song, gripping a branch with one hand, leaning out, and waving with the other. "Was that your exit?" She pointed the direction of the opening in the side of the ship.

"Yes," Falco called. "Aldrik was with us. Have you seen him?"

"Seen him?" Song laughed, pushing her dark hair back from her face. Her clothing was dirty on one side, as if she'd landed at the bottom of a well, but otherwise, she appeared sound. "He saved me. I was about to go over, and the man rammed me with his chair. He's up here probing the area with his LiDAR, searching for the others."

"Any luck?"

Falco stepped into the clearing to answer her, and Saana let him have his lead, while she headed the opposite direction. The undergrowth was rustling, and she moved toward the shifting leaves. Pushing a fern aside, beneath the waving fronds she found the Acolyte, the boy who traveled with the Bishop. He was on his knees, his head bowed, and his hands in an attitude of prayer.

"Boy, are you injured? Has your god protected you?" She didn't see what his god might have to do with anything, but she didn't see any blood, either. It seemed like a thing My Sister might ask, and she encouraged Saana's empathetic side regularly. Perhaps it was the boy's youth that prompted her to give in and ask the question.

"Shush!" He held his rolled hand to his chin,

two fingers on his lips, and he pulled her down to kneel at his side. "His Excellency is just through there—" pointing into the undergrowth "—and will return shortly."

"Is he . . . incapacitated?" Saana stood, placed her cupped hand to her mouth, and drew in a breath to call.

"No!" The boy grabbed her arm, immediately crossing himself and bowing his head respectfully. "I humbly apologize, mistress. I meant no offense."

"None taken. Why can't I—" The question was interrupted by the appearance of the Bishop, pushing through the undergrowth and adjusting his clothing. His eyes were down, and she was sure he wasn't aware of her presence.

"My child, I'm afraid I came unprepared for something so crude as what I've just experienced." He wiped something from his foot onto the grassy surface. "I was forced to use leaves. I pray to God I'm not allergic to anything on this world." He glanced up, and seeing they weren't alone, paled and gulped.

"My Bishop, we have company." The boy stood and dropped his head respectfully, his face disappearing into the folds of his hood. He turned to Saana, his face shadowed, and whispered, "You may speak with the His Excellency now, if you wish."

CASK

"I . . . I . . ." Bishop Zubizarreta looked back the way he'd come, glanced down, and wiped his foot once more, then bowed his head briskly in a small motion and cleared his throat. "Engineer Ssanyu, I believe. You seem well. Our ship has expelled us, for what sins, I do not know. Are we gathering somewhere?" His face brightened, and he looked her eagerly in the eyes. "A rescue craft. Has someone notified Rome of my situation? I'm certain Rome will send help as soon as it can be comfortably arranged."

"I pray that it will be so." She hoped My Sister appreciated her words. They weren't in her heart, even if they came from her mouth. "This way, please, Bishop. Your boy, also. Captain Falco waits, as does First Mate Song. I believe we will join Science Officer Jollenbeck in short order. Are you aware of any others who managed to escape the ship with you?"

"Nay, mistress." The Acolyte shifted his hood until his face was partially exposed. His cheeks were smooth, that of a youth who had yet to put a razor to his beard. "River . . . er, First Mate Song rendered us aid and pointed the way to the exit. We saw no one else along the way."

"Child! Respect! Familiarity is not allowed." The Bishop patted his robes, his hands feeling his pockets, and his eyes blinking in concern. "My talisman! I cannot find my talisman!"

"Your Excellency, if I may." The Acolyte stepped forward, gently worked his hand at the Bishop's throat, lifted the red talisman from the Bishop's clothing, and released it gently to shimmer with an internal light on the man's breast.

"In the name of the Father, the Son, and the Holy Ghost, I thought it lost." He looked into the heavens and made the sign of the Cross over his torso. He shifted his attention to Ssanyu and smiled, opening his hands in a welcoming fashion, his palms up. "My good Engineer, I suppose we must trust you to lead us. We are lost in all things."

"Except in doing the Will of God, for there is no shadow of misdirection in Him," the Acolyte murmured, his head bowed, displaying an image of respectful subservience to his master.

"Amen," the Bishop agreed.

"The globe, is it functional?" Saana had not realized there was a Thracian Globe on board. It lay to the side, and she knew, without the ship's power, it might come in handy. They might make it to the city before dark, if they were fortunate, but perhaps not.

"And a second." The Acolyte withdrew one from his robe. "Shall I carry them with us?"

"Good boy." The child smiled, and Saana almost patted his head. He glanced at the Bishop, and his smile fell away. She knew she was right to speak kindly to him when she felt My Sister stir inside, and her whispered words emerged for the briefest moment, a sparkling and effervescent sprinkling of thoughts bursting against the tumbling turmoil of their shared consciousness. *You are learning.* Saana felt the words warm her, and that in itself left her irritated. She barked, "We must move. Bishop, follow me, if you will. Boy, bring your globes."

"Yes, mistress," he said, nodding, his face once again disappearing within his robe.

"Captain?" Saana called as she pulled the foliage aside and stepped into the clearing. It was empty. "Song?" The branch was bare. "Jollenbeck?" They had left them. She wasn't worried, for their disappearance was of little consequence. She would find them. It was what she did. As she turned to ensure her two hangers-on were following, the branches behind the Bishop cracked and parted, to reveal three angry Army soldiers burdened by the Envoy's Cask. Medical Officer Franklin was on their heels. His normally friendly face spouted a frown, as he pulled a shoe off one foot.

"Wildlife! I would step in the only scat this side of St. Petersburg! Just my luck!" He leaned against a tree on one foot and wiped the sole of his shoe against the bark. Shaking his head, he slipped the shoe on and stood erect, brushing at his pants to line up the creases. He touched the Med-Tab at his throat and said softly, "Research: local fauna capable of humanoid-type feces."

The Acolyte was smiling, and the Bishop's face was red. Saana understood perfectly. She shifted the scene, calling, "Doctor Franklin, the Envoy is well?"

"Ah, Toofer. You made it, as did Preach and Ditto. Hello, boy. Thracian Globes? Fascinating things." He clasped the boy's shoulder in a friendly way. The Acolyte's face was hidden, so Saana couldn't see his response, but he seemed to stand taller. "Engineer Ssanyu, I wish to convey my gratitude for the unquestioned help of Buster, Search, and Loki. They've been invaluable with the Envoy. Astonishingly good fellows."

The doctor's smile seemed to include them all. Saana recognized the nicknames. Buster was the soldier, Ghost. Search and Loki were Recon and Pyro. Toofer? That was her—she supposed because there were two of them in this head of theirs. It was an affectionate name, and she didn't mind it from the doctor. She turned to see Jollenbeck's wheelchair break through the growth behind her, his body encased in electronic armor, except for his head and shoulders. His Aakash chattered amiably, with green humor scattered across the screen, the sine waves reflecting his animated speech, his arrival shadowed by the Captain and his First Mate.

"Has the Android arrived?" Captain Falco cut

to the chase, asking the pointed question. It was valid, his choice of words more beneficial to the situation than any words of greeting, no matter how socially adroit, could be. The Android was their most versatile tool, able to morph into any shape or thing they needed, and more importantly, possessing the ability to uplink to passing vessels and register a distress signal.

"That spider thing?" Recon spat the words. "Nah, probably still crawling the underbelly of the ship."

"Now's not the time," Ghost barked, holding out a hand, his palm down. To his side, Pyro's face hardened for a moment. His eyes glanced at the Cask and jerked away again. The animosity could be stirred with a stick.

Saana wondered which man would begin to stir it first.

—Chapter 16—

Dreadnaught *Vladimir Vladimirovich Putin*

Flight Command Technician Kai Kumar
. . . in which a slight unseen can never be unheard

*SENSORS CALIBRATION and Flight Command
Systems Technician.* Kai Kumar stood outside his
quarters, his heart pounding and his head filled
with explosive ordnance, and he repeated his title.
*Sensors Calibration and Flight Command Systems
Technician.* "That's me," he whispered, with a bit
of a wheeze after his final word. "Do you guys
think I don't know what you say when you think
I'm not around?"

Kumar wiped a meaty palm against the leg of
his uniform to remove the stickiness of a pastry
he'd finished on the way from the Mess. He pushed
himself from the wall and pressed his hand to the
sensor, relieved when the door moved a slight
distance and sealed itself with a pneumatic suction.

Technician Kumar. He hated the name. It said

nothing. Anyone could be a technician. Look at Mohamed. Sewer duty. Or Korhonen. What was his purpose on the ship? Numbers. Data collection. How important was that? And Hansen working with computers all day, although Kumar couldn't fault him too much for that. The computers did keep the ship operational, though he couldn't see that Hansen did all that much. Any AI could handle everything Hansen did, and probably more efficiently.

But *sensors calibration.* How important was that? The doors aboard the ship wouldn't open without Kumar's expertise. Like the one to his quarters. He'd set it to open just a few centimeters so he could check if anyone was inside before he entered. Just for him, that was all. It only did it for his hand, not for anyone else's, and that was his doing. Lock someone out of the system? He could do that, too, even the Captain if he wanted.

Better not, though. He chuckled, looking up and down the corridor, relieved there was no one.

He also controlled the flight command systems, well, not *controlled,* but he could. Set them the way he wanted, altering the course at any point in the journey, fouling up everyone's schedule. It would be easy, even though he'd never do it. He thought about it, though. If he wanted, he could be the most powerful person on the ship.

He *was* the most powerful person, even if he

chose not to exercise that power.

He could, though. He could. He had heard Korhonen. "A man we can respect." And he knew he wasn't talking about him. Mori. That's the man he could respect, and why? Because his brain would fall out without his titanium alloy plate. Pshaw. That was nothing. Mori would probably be as useful without his brain as he was with it. Pilot-in-Command. What was a pilot-in-command? Less than a technician, in Kumar's estimation. And Mori would be given command of the Bridge if they engaged in a Cygnian offensive.

It was not fair for those with less ability to have more authority. It wasn't fair even a bit.

Kumar took a deep breath, felt only a small stitch in his side, and decided he was recovered enough to move away from his quarters and find another place to rest. He shifted his bulk from the wall, adjusted his balance, and wondered if there was anything to eat in the recreation area, and then he remembered. It wasn't a recreation area any longer. Agrippa's *team* had taken it over, and Kumar had been assigned to bunk with Hansen and Korhonen, and now they thought *Pilot-in-Command* Mori was the best thing ever, and Kumar had nowhere to go, not anywhere he wanted to go, anyway. Hydroponics, maybe, but all they had was lettuce and tomatoes. Who wanted lettuce and tomatoes? He needed something with more flavor than lettuce and tomatoes. He couldn't help it if his body had special dietary needs. Who could be skinny when you were always hungry, and hungry for real food, like pastries and gravy and pasta?

"Kai?"

The voice caught Kumar off guard, and he turned abruptly, nearly stumbling. Communications Systems Technician Dasha Ivanova walked confidently his way, moving at a faster clip than Kumar thought appropriate for any normal person aboard the *Putin*. She wore a thin, moisture-wicking towel around her neck.

"Dasha." Kumar hugged the side of the corridor, expecting her to walk on by, and his heart pounded when she slowed. What did she want? "Are you heading to the gym?" He'd seen the towel, and it was where she spent much of her free time.

"Returning. You look peaked. Aren't your temporary quarters near here?" She glanced at the various doors, then pointed. "That one, right?" She smiled and didn't seem unfriendly.

"It's full up right now. I was headed to Recreation when I remembered it's not recreation any longer." He shrugged, thinking of the pastry he'd finished earlier. He wondered if he could return to the Mess without seeming piggish. If he waited an hour or two, the changeover in personnel would disguise his repeat appearance. Was this too soon?

"Right. Briefing." She snorted, wrinkling her nose. "Glad they left my quarters alone. So, you're with Soren and Ziggy for this trip, right?" She glanced at the door she'd indicated, as if she might be interested in going in.

"And Mori. He's the pilot-in-command for the duration of our deployment. He's in there now, and that's why I didn't go in." Kumar pressed his lips together hard, angry at the *team* that had compromised the crew's quarters aboard the *Putin*. "Playing something called Mölkky." He shifted his bulk, aware of the tightness of his uniform next to Ivanova's svelte shape.

"Oh." Ivanova's shoulders sagged just a bit, then she laughed in a short, quick burst. "You've been invaded by the foreigners that have come to command our ship to a bigger victory against the Cygnian fleet."

"Well, only if we run into one of their ships, so maybe not. Our real job is to intercept the *Roosevelt,* something to do with the Envoy it's carrying." Kumar shrugged. It was like Ivanova to take the wind out of his sails. She was always about *Dasha*, and traumas aboard ship never seemed to bother her much. He wanted sympathy, not a bright outlook on events that felt traumatic to him.

"And you feel left out. Your shipmates

preferring the new boy over you." She stroked his arm, consoling him, giving her bottom lip a bit of a pout.

"I don't even understand Mölkky. Who wants to play a game they can't understand, anyway?" Kumar didn't know if she was humoring him or truly understood the travesty of his situation.

"Mölkky's a tough nut to crack. Soren tried to teach me for several hours a while back, and either I have no patience for it, or he's a lousy teacher. Hey, Kai, I've got something I want to show you. Are you interested?" She lifted the corner of her towel and patted one side of her forehead.

"Um, maybe. It's not at the gym, is it?" No way did he want to see anything there.

"You mean this." She pulled the towel from her neck and folded it in half. "I was doing a power-walk as a cooldown. You look like you could use a pick-me-up, and I have just the thing."

"You have a pastry?" Ivanova was culturally Russian, and Kumar pictured a Chocolate Salami or a Napoleon Cake. Perhaps the sponge-and-mousse Bird's Milk Cake.

"I wish, but sadly, no. This is better. Come, Kai. I will treat you as you've never been treated." She wrapped her towel—nearly dry and exuding the fresh scent of a Russian meadow in the spring—around his neck and gently tugged on it.

"Nothing sexual, Dasha. I'll come, but I won't

do that." Ivanova was very attractive, with her dark hair and pronounced features, but Kumar didn't want to become the butt of the stories that he knew went around when he wasn't there.

"Oh, you!" She pulled the towel free and patted his face, not unkindly. "Why do men always think with their third leg? I want you to tell me a story, that's all. Maybe about Soren and Ziggy. What do the cousins do in their free time? Maybe you can tell me that?"

"That's all you want?" He felt doubt squeeze his chest.

"You do know something, don't you? Now that you share quarters with them, I'm sure you have all sorts of good stories you can share." She had her arm entwined with his, and they were moving— slowly, at that—away from Kumar's quarters.

"Some things." He glanced back to his door receding into the corridor. He couldn't beg off to return there, with *"a man we can respect"* ringing in his ears, and there was no place else to go until the Mess had time to change out to a new group of diners.

"So, we're set, then."

"What is it you really want, Dasha?" Kumar stopped, bracing his feet against the tug of her arm.

"Just stories." She smiled beguilingly.

"And you want to show me what?"

"Oh, Kai." She huffed and pulled her arm free.

"Surely even you know about my still. You do know what a still is?"

"You make ethanol, sure. I've heard some people mention it."

"I make whiskey, not ethanol. Well, one and the same, I guess, but mine is whiskey, specifically, and I'll share it with you for one of your stories. You just have to make a good one, okay? You need to make this worth my time."

"Worth your time. For a story about Soren."

"Or Ziggy." She giggled. "Preferably something wicked."

"Wicked." Kumar wondered if she'd know if he made something up. He wasn't sure Soren or Ziggy was particularly wicked, except to him, and that was mostly ignoring him when he was around.

Then he remembered something he'd overheard Korhonen mumbling in his sleep in the middle of the night, something about a terrorist organization and wondering if the money was worth it to bleed information about the ship's activities during her deployment. He didn't know more than that, but he could certainly fill in interesting details.

"Okay, I've got something," he said. His head was muddled up with *"a man we can respect"* and Mori. Yes, he thought he could come up with something really good, wicked, that is, and the great thing is that it would be completely true, well, some of it would.

"And it's wicked?" She grinned and wrapped her arm back in his.

"Maybe." He shrugged, refusing to commit, while he moved his feet, this time willingly, assembling his story as he walked.

"I hope so. Do you know that someday I plan to captain a private ship?"

"Private ship?"

"Don't repeat me, Kai. This is from my heart, something important to me. I want a private salvage ship of my own, you know, explore the far reaches of the Solar System with no one to tell me my duty cycle, never see my name on a duty roster, and go where I want to go."

"Oh, wow." Kumar hadn't thought about anyone ever wanting to do that.

"And I'll tell you more if your story about Soren and Ziggy is really good . . ."

CASK

—Chapter 17—

Interdicted Colony World *Verboten*

The Acolyte

. . . in which an original thought wins a friend

IT IS MY DESIRE in life to be unnoticed, so speaks the Will of God. It is my desire in life to be unnoticed, so speaks our Holy God. It is my desire in life to be noticed . . . oh, forgive me, Excellency. What am I thinking? *I* desire to be unnoticed. The Bishop will have me washing his underwear again tonight—twice!—if I continue in my errant thoughts. I must not think such things.

At a sound in the trees, the soldiers broke through the greenery, so exciting! This had become a day like no other, filled with adventure. They had the Envoy with them, carrying him on their shoulders. Bishop, move, I wanted to cry, as I cannot see the Abomination for your holy wideness.

"My Son," Bishop Zubizarreta gave me a reprimanding scowl, causing me to cringe, "you must not push. To be forceful is to place yourself above others, and such is a sin."

"Yes, your Holy Worship." Still, I could not see. This whole trip, the Envoy, the alien, has been aboard our ship, and not once, not once have I been allowed so much as a glimpse.

I was warmed by the attention of the two-person Engineer. She seemed very satisfied with my globes, and I wished I carried more to please her. I am often spoken to kindly by the two-person one, more so when Bishop Zubizarreta is about other business.

First Mate Song called to us from the clearing. She shared with me one evening over a cup of delicious cocoa the meaning of her true name. In her parent language, her name translates as River Dynasty, a most beautiful sound, and I told her so. She confided in me that the meaning was for me, alone, and I wasn't to share it with anyone. I have told only the Bishop, for I'm not allowed to keep secrets from God, nor from the Bishop. He is my spiritual example, and I must emulate him wholeheartedly, although sometimes I must quiet my inner self when the Bishop is indiscreet in his morning toilet. I quote the Prayer of the Sinner until he is finished, and I feel as though I am a better person afterward.

I barely contained my pleasure when the doctor called my name, although I know it is a sin. I'm not to call attention to myself, but the Bishop can hardly fault me, when I have made myself as inconspicuous as possible, and yet I am noticed by another. When the doctor spoke of the animal scat, the Bishop caught my eye and gave me a stern look. I have vowed to forget the reason for the Bishop's trip into the trees, as if it never happened. If someone should ask me, my thoughts will be blank.

No one knew what to do, not even the soldiers, for they seemed as confused as any of us. The arrival of Officer Jollenbeck, or Cryp, as he is often called by Doctor Franklin, jarred our group into action. The Captain asked a pointed question about the location of the ship's false person, the Android. I have spoken to this false person on several occasions, most frequently when on errands for the Bishop, and I find him fascinating. How can a machine contain the words and manners of a man, yet easily become any shape it desires, and change back again? It confuses me, and yet, when I speak with him, I find myself curious to discover his motivations and dreams, whether he is more like me than different, and whether he has a soul. If he were to wear human skin, I'd not know him from any other person on this ship, as machine or human. It clouds my thoughts, and I hope he's not lost.

As the Acolyte looked around, everyone except

the Android was present. If humans survived the ship's forced landing, surely a machine of the Android's professed capabilities wouldn't suffer damage. He was dismayed to hear the soldier (Recon, his helmet said) refer to the Android as a spider thing. It struck too strong a chord with the boy, and he'd already resolved to make up his own mind in the matter.

"First, we must locate the ship's Android, then we need to make our way downward." Captain Falco spoke with authority, drawing them into a common endeavor. The Acolyte admired his skill, something he would never have in such abundance.

"Um, will there be transportation?" The Bishop raised a hand tentatively, as if afraid he would be ignored. The group paused as a whole and turned to him. "The gravity . . . I feel so very heavy. Surely we're not expected to walk all the way. And my things, I must have my prayer books, my Holy Cross of the Crypt, and my case of sacraments from the ship. They have been blessed by the Holy Father. It's the reason I'm here, the Unalterable and Holy Will of the Father. The Religious Right to Unity desires conversion of the Envoy, and my mission will fail otherwise." He smiled pleadingly.

Recon, the soldier who made the unpleasant remark earlier, was most disgusting, and the boy felt some of his admiration for him wane. He retracted his faceplate and spat loudly on the grass, barely missing the Envoy's Cask. His companions, Ghost and Pyro, laughed; but the Acolyte supposed they felt obligated to support their team member. He was required to do the same for Bishop Zubizarreta, even when he didn't agree with his opinions. The Bishop felt the Android could not have a soul, and was an abomination, no matter how kind he was to the boy when they spoke. For this reason, he couldn't allow himself to judge Ghost and Pyro until he knew their motivations better.

Officer Song replied kindly to the Bishop, for which the Acolyte was appreciative. "Bishop, as you can see, the fire suppressant has filled the ship. There is no way inside until it liquefies, which might be hours or even days in this dense atmosphere. If we find transportation in the city, perhaps we can return later to retrieve your personal things."

"I . . . um, suppose that must do. I do have my talisman, and for that I can be grateful." He fingered the ruby necklace, and as he turned, he nearly stumbled. The Acolyte felt fortunate to be at his side and to catch his arm.

"I have you, Your Excellency." He kept his head low and his face covered, for he was ashamed of his thoughts. He carried within his robes the things the Bishop required, and a surge of pride had overtaken him for a moment. The Bishop had forgotten that he gathered his prayer books and the Holy Cross of the Crypt, although he was unable to manage the sacraments. Now was not the time to remind him, as he would be calling attention to himself, and he suspected that the Bishop, should he be humiliated in front of the Envoy, would, in his wisdom, find even more pairs of underwear for the boy to wash before the night was through.

"Ssanya, you and Prime—" Captain Falco didn't get a chance to complete his instructions, for a panel in the side of the ship flew into the air with a metallic tearing sound, and an unusual looking metallic shape covered with remnants of yellow fire-suppressant foam accompanied it.

"Captain," Jollenbeck's Aakash signaled in warning, as the sine waves on the device compressed tightly together. His Aakash glowed blue, which the Acolyte had been told revealed a measure of confidence in his current situation. "Incoming!"

The boy glanced up, pulling his hood from his head, to fully see what happened. In flight, before landing, the metallic shape shifted to take the form of a man, with shimmering arms, legs, and a head. There was no skin, for the Android always wore his metal as a testament to his otherness, and so that no one would confuse him for a flesh-born man. The Acolyte didn't see his metal-ness as arrogance, for he sensed no pride in him, only kindness, and goodwill to those aboard the ship. When it seemed he would land near to the boy's location, he stepped aside to allow him room. The Bishop fell heavily to his knees before his companion could take his elbow, and he grasped his talisman with both hands, bowing his head and repeating a mumbled prayer. Around them, the crewmembers of the ship smiled in anticipation, while the soldiers kept their hands tensed in tight fists.

The gleaming metal man landed heavily in front of the Bishop, crouched, his feet buried partially in the soil. He stood and apologized to Bishop Zubizarreta, requesting his patience, explaining that it was difficult to choose an accurate trajectory while his body was in transformation. The Acolyte thrilled at the metal man's revelation and was dismayed to hear His Holiness whisper, "Abomination!"

The Acolyte hadn't yet made up his mind that such a kind person, although perhaps false, as the Bishop suggested, could truly be soulless, so he stepped to him, dropped his head respectfully, and said, "I'm glad you're safe. You're welcome to journey with us to the city below. I will be glad to assist you, if I can."

He dared not look at the Bishop, and he resigned himself to washing His Worship's underwear three times once they arrived at their destination. It would be worth it. No creature deserves to be cruelly cast aside, especially one that had treated him with respect on multiple occasions. He was surprised to feel a hand on his shoulder. His eye caught a metallic gleam. He looked up to the Android's sculpted, silver-black face watching his. His red eyes shimmered—tears, surely not—and his voice was gentle as he spoke.

"I will be proud to walk at your side."

Captain Falco began to speak, but the Acolyte had no idea what he said, only that their group was organizing, and after a time, they began to move through the understory down the hillside and toward the city. Even the Bishop's glowering look couldn't diminish the thoughts running over and over in his head.

Ship's Android is proud to walk at my side . . . at *my* side!

CASK

—Chapter 18—

Dreadnaught *Vladimir Vladimirovich Putin*

Second Engineer Lilou Apinelu
. . . in which a rug is meant to be stepped on

LILOU APINELU SAT AT HER STATION on the Bridge, her hands pausing over the capacitive touch screens covering her work surface. Her glass tablet was off to the side, and she glanced at it before tapping out a series of commands on the screens.

Kazlauskas, she thought. *You idiot.*

As Second Engineer, responsible for propulsion and the FTL drives, this was her first outspace mission, and she was well aware her advancement hinged on her performance. When Captain Devi had ordered them to clear the Bridge, Apinelu had returned and decided Kazlauskas had tripped the circuits purposely to foul up Apinelu's day.

A red circle flashed on one panel, and Apinelu's earbud screeched. She grimaced and looked around the Bridge to see if anyone had noticed. First Mate Murphy was in the Chair. Apinelu always said it with a capital C. Her first time out, remember. The Chair. It was a very auspicious fixture on the bridge of a starship. Murphy had his nose in a virtual screen hovering in front of his face, and he reached and tapped something invisible to Apinelu. Helmsman Quispe was still on watch, although he was surely about to go off duty, allowing the thick-necked Papadopoulos to take his place. Quispe whispered into a microphone, clearly unaware of the noise in Apinelu's earbud. Navigator John, with her thick tangle of hair, tapped away at a capacitive touch screen of her own, the colors surging through geometric patterns telling the woman of something Apinelu didn't understand.

Apinelu was certain they were all in contact with one another, using their Transdermal Communication Devices, something she, as a firstie, wasn't privy to. She had her tablet, lah-te-dah. She was relieved that the screech through her earbud seemed under the radar, so to speak, something Kazlauskas had better be grateful for. The Third Engineer was no more than a stepping-stone, as far as Apinelu was concerned, and if she screwed with her, Apinelu would happily toss her out of the airlock.

Glancing at her tablet again, she tried to

override the warning by tapping the red circle. It faded, and her earbud quieted, but as soon as she put that part of the panel in background mode, the circle reappeared, and the screeching started up again.

"What the—" Apinelu yanked the bud from her ear and grimaced. It had been louder the second time.

"Engineer?" A hand clasped her shoulder gently.

"What?" She turned abruptly, to find First Engineer Rodriguez at her side. The graybeard raised his eyebrows at her sharp response. "Sorry, sir. I just had an alarm sound twice in my ear."

"And in mine." He nodded at her display, and it was obvious he didn't wear an earbud. TCDs. Clearly, he had heard it over the Net using his Transdermal Communication Device. "As this is the second time, perhaps you can discover the cause for the alarm."

"Yessir." Apinelu faced her console and closed her eyes just for a moment. Rodriguez. If she had a boss aboard, Rodriguez was it. She hoped this didn't knock down her chances for a quick advancement once this mission was over. She brought up the offending section of the display to fill the panel, and she touched it, feeling the subtle haptic feedback through the capacitive touch screen. A keyboard appeared just below the warning symbol, and Apinelu began to type in instructions. The warning symbol faded to a schematic of the ship's drives. After several keystrokes, the image pulled in, narrowing the view of the drives, with the red dot still displayed, just smaller. Apinelu paused when the image and the dot moved without her input.

"Okay, sir. That's not what I expected." She reached for her tablet.

"Oh? How so?" Rodriguez's voice was calm, even ominously neutral. Apinelu glanced at him before setting her tablet down.

"If there's an error, sir, the system should have it pinned down to one location. That's how the warning works."

"And?"

"Did you see—" The screen shifted again before she could finish her question. Then again, the image tracking what appeared to be an internal electrical conduit, essentially the neural pathway of the drive system's electronic brain.

"I see it." Rodriguez's voice tightened, as if he really wanted to discover what this was.

"Let me try this, sir." Apinelu tapped several times on her tablet, wishing she had access to the ship's Net. Accessing what she needed by tablet was so cumbersome as to be stone age. A window opened, and she scrolled down to a series of instructions. She typed them into the larger display,

CASK

her fingers blurring with speed.

The display flipped, twisted, and widened, cutting off much of the information. What was left was a red dot that moved with a degree of intelligence, although at the current resolution, it was merely *there*, even though its motions were apparent.

"I want identification, Apinelu. Work your magic."

"Yessir." Apinelu accepted that Rodriguez held all the keys in her endeavor to achieve a quick promotion off the *Putin* and onto a more important ship, but his areas of expertise were the structural and mechanical framework of the ship. He was the crew's EVA Specialist, but even that didn't eclipse her own area of specialty. She might be forced to work from a tablet, but she knew the propulsion systems aboard the *Putin* like no one else, and she could make it jump to her demands, if she had to fire her electronic six-shooters directly at its feet.

Apinelu typed, and the image shifted again, pulling in tighter. The error was still a red circle, but the image of the schematics was tight enough they could see the circle shifting into alternate pathways, doing something potentially ominous, and pulling out again to continue its journey of . . . whatever.

"I think we have a ghost, sir." Apinelu reached to her tablet, touched it several times, then studied what was on the screen. "Let me try this."

She pressed a combination of keys, forcing the keyboard to shift to something only an engineer of faster-than-light propulsion systems would see as anything other than squiggles on the display. She hit a number of them in rapid succession, and it was like water washed over the display. She sat back and let the computer do its thing for a minute. It looked like an old-fashioned darkroom image as the computer extrapolated information, kicked out extraneous bytes, and determined where the anomaly had originated and where it had been. It took most of that minute before the water cleared and a label appeared on the red dot.

al-D.CSO.UCC.

"Sir?" Apinelu pointed to the display where the label now tracked alongside the red dot. It shifted as they watched, moving along a pathway that Apinelu recognized as the aorta of the propulsion system, leading directly to the FTL drives. It stopped and remained still for a time.

"Why did it stop?" Rodriguez revealed his level of concern by tapping the screen where the red dot pulsed steadily, as if trying to get past a blockage.

"Sir, let me help." Apinelu fought a smile. The answer was obvious—to her, at least—and being able to explain would chalk up plenty of gold stars for her, she was certain. "There's an electronic gate there, and without a special code, nothing can get through. Not even the ship's AI. That's an area too sensitive to trust to cybernetic lifeforms."

"And the code is where?" Rodriguez seemed to be putting something together.

"Here." Apinelu tapped her temple. "And only here."

"U. C. C." He said it slowly, as if the code no longer mattered. "That rings a bell. Engineer?" The Chief Officer gnawed the edge of one lip, just enough to be apparent.

"UCC? Oh, that's easy." Apinelu blinked twice. She hadn't recognized it on the monitor, but when the Chief asked it like that, the answer jumped into her head. "Updatable Cybernetic Construct."

"And al-D. How about that one, Engineer? Ring any bells?" He stood and chuckled, now more confident.

"Um, al-Din, with Agrippa?" Her eyes widened. She had heard the guest team were enhanced, even beyond what the *Putin* crew had available. If they could do this—

"I believe this stands for al-Din, Combat Systems Officer, Updatable Cybernetic Construct. Now, I wonder, Engineer, why would one of our visitors' updatable cybernetic constructs be exploring our propulsion system?"

"Not for a good reason, sir. That'd be my

guess." Apinelu studied the label on the screen, the red dot it was attached to exploring as she watched.

"I think you'd be right, Engineer. Are you certain it can't do any damage?"

"Pretty sure, sir, unless they have Uppernet capability we can't sense. Then, all bets would be off."

"You monitor that, and I'll keep your suggestion in mind. I'll be letting Murphy and the Captain know about this."

She turned to her console as he walked away, expecting that with his access to the ship's Net through his Transdermal Communication Device, he already had. Never mind that, she wanted to be able to do what al-Din could do.

She now wanted a UCC more than anything, and she'd walk over anyone on board the ship if that ever became an option.

CASK

Chapter 19

Interdicted Colony World *Verboten*

Captain Vicente Falco
. . . looks forward to sticks and stones

"PYRO. OR DO YOU prefer Loki?" Loki was Doctor Franklin's name for the soldier at my side. I'd heard him answer to it numerous times.

"Either." His word came out with a shrug.

I looked at the soldier as we made our way down the hillside. How a man could shrug with his voice alone, I had no idea. I could see little of him. He, as did the other two, remained fully suited, bristling with weapons and munitions. Even his face was covered by his glass-fronted helmet, the light inside painting his skin green. I wondered whether the suits had an integrated exoskeleton. The three soldiers were carrying the Cask with the Envoy inside, the balloon wheels just off the ground, and that was no mean feat. I'd struggle to lift even a corner, and I'm not a small man.

Okay, I decided. This wasn't the time to rock the boat. Ours had crashed, and if we found another one, I wanted us all on board. Together. As a team. The man had Pyro stenciled on his helmet, so that was it.

"Pyro, then. May I speak freely?" He'd take what I had to say better, if he agreed to go along.

"You're the Captain." He turned his head slightly my direction, and I caught his eyes. Under the green light, it gave the whites an odd cast. Freaky, but then, for a soldier, I guess freaky is a good thing.

"Right, I'm the Captain. I'm not unreasonable, though."

"Never thought you were. What'cha need to say? I'm all ears." He continued to walk and talk, even downhill, with no apparent effort. I could use that sort of strength. I was slipping on the grass, having to watch every step, and this man seemed to be casually strolling.

"I was surprised to see you three carrying the Cask. The Envoy's not on Ghost's register of best-liked people."

"Don't know that Ghost thinks of it as people." He paused, looking ahead, then added, "Sir."

"So, why . . . if you don't mind?" I shrugged as if it didn't matter, but I really was curious. I noticed the other two keeping track of us, Recon with his blue light, and Ghost with red; and it occurred to me, they could probably hear every word. I was confident the suits had internal comms. It only made sense, militarily.

"Doctor Franklin's a good man. We respect him, sir." Again, that slight pause, as if the sir was for effect, not respect.

"And he asked you." I looked for Richard and found him at Science Officer Jollenbeck's side, along with Prime. The chair was having difficulty, even with the oversized wheels we'd attached. I suspected Aldrik would rather use his magnetic lift and skim over all these obstacles. I wished I'd been insistent on upgrading his Tesla reactor. He'd have all the power he needed, then. Still, we'd already crossed that threshold. No going backwards, not in my book.

"He did, and we stepped up. It's what the Army does." I caught his lips, and they were pressed in a straight line. I also didn't get a sir that time, not like it was skin off my back.

"Thank you, Pyro. I suspect you're a good man, too." I wasn't sure, but speak positive words and get positive results. I've always believed that, and I hoped it was true now. I didn't need the Army turning on me in our current situation.

"If you say so, sir. May I?" He nodded straight ahead, and I dropped away. I smiled. I got my sir back.

The sky had begun to cloud up, and I felt the

first raindrops hit. We'd neared the bottom of the hill, and the trees had thinned, leaving a vast swath of waist-high grasses, all the way to the city. Why didn't these people build roads? I wondered. Glancing behind me to ensure we were together, my ship was just visible, a small section catching a lone ray of light through the undergrowth. Trees, massive and green, had eaten my wonderful beauty. The ridgeline was a jagged jawline of pointed teeth, sharp and deadly, snapping falling ships out of the air before they could safely land. The *Roosevelt* had been ripped from the sky, food for a god of soil, air, and trees. I took a breath and reached out for something more practical to occupy my thoughts.

"Bishop," I called, watching the man struggle alone. He was one of the last in line and having difficulty, most of it coming from lifting his skirts to keep them dry from the damp grasses. His shoulders were dotted with raindrops. If we didn't get to the city soon, he'd have more than just raindrops to suffer through.

"The grace of the Holy Father is my strength, Captain. With God's faithful love in my arms and legs, I'll make it. I will, I'm certain." He panted, then wheezed, grabbing his chest, "The gravity, Captain. How can the gravity be so strong? I can hardy breathe."

"The air's thicker. You've a boy with you for

assistance—"

"A wastrel, a failure! An abject failure!" The Bishop stopped walking and looked skyward. "I told the Holy Father the boy wasn't prepared. Experience, I pleaded. Send me someone with strong arms and a stronger conscience. No," and he looked at me as though it were my fault, "they saddle me with an incompetent boy, and he does nothing—nothing right, anyway." He began to walk again, although at a slower pace. The rain had become steady, though light, and his hems were taking on water. He continued to hold them heavenward, though little good I could see from it.

"He could aid you. Let me—"

"Leave him." He brushed my concern away and took the ruby crystal at his throat, holding it tightly. "I get more help from my talisman than from that boy. He's taken up with the . . . the . . . silver thing." He blustered the word, barely able to get it out.

The boy was in an animated discussion with the Android, more spirited than I'd seen him on the whole voyage. They'd noticed Aldrik's troubles and joined him, working his chair delicately over rocks and other debris. We were lost without the Android . . . and the boy? If he chose the Android as his friend, he'd likely turn out just fine, indeed.

"Thank you, Bishop. I have others I need to see. If you don't mind?" I nodded at him and moved towards Jollenbeck's chair.

"Captain?"

"Yes, Bishop?" I turned, even as my feet carried me on. What more could this man want?

"Send the boy to me, if you don't mind. It's his duty to be at my side."

"Of course. Anything else?"

"Just the boy." The Bishop panted, his hands on his knees, and his face red with exertion.

I failed to watch my own feet, and down I went, into a small hole. I stood, now wet and muddy. It didn't help when all three soldiers looked my way, red, green, and blue. They turned from me, with no emotion and no offer of help. I was fine, so it was as well. It was Engineer Ssanyu that twisted my gut. I'm sure it was Sanaa who called, "Captain, walk this way, if you wish to remain erect." She was lifting her feet in a dramatic marching step, and she laughed.

"Certainly, Sanaa. You're very kind." In reality, I was ready for some stone floors under my feet and sticks and boards for a covering overhead. Being outdoors appeals to some people, but my bones need something more.

CASK

—Chapter 20—

Dreadnaught *Vladimir Vladimirovich Putin*

al-Din – Updatable Cybernetic Construct
. . . in which a hot time in the wires makes for a good day

[[Hot! Hot!]] al-D.CSO.UCC zipped along the fiberlines of the *Vladimir Vladimirovich Putin*, repeating the words to herself, [[Hot! Hot!]]

As a cybernetic construct, nothing was better than the sensation of speed that she equated with heat, like the surge of an old-fashioned roller coaster, the wheels grasping the rails, the friction building as each wheel passed, cool at the front, and hotter, hotter, hotter as each wheel covered the distance the linked cars traveled.

[[Hot! Hot!]] al-D shivered in anticipation at each new junction in the fiberlines. The electrical conduits were her life, what she was constructed to do, gather, gather, gather, explore, explore, explore, then gather some more. The only thing better than the sizzle of the lines as she flung her cybernetic body along their unfettered length was merging with her other half during the long dark times when the CSO's material meat and jelly body was at rest, her brain paused in time-out mode, readied by design and attenuation to absorb everything the Construct had ferreted out during the daylight hours.

As if the Construct ever saw the light of day.

Except she did! She did! There! She tapped at an electronic gate, sending across an electric impulse to open, with no results. She tried another impulse, different yet the same, then another, patient, patient, patient. Ten thousand attempts later (no more than a nanosecond, at most) and the gate tripped open, letting al-D inside. The lines had cooled as she waited, and she was ready to move, move, move once more.

[[Hot! Hot!]] she sighed in relief as she picked up speed again. She recognized where she was. The electronic gate had murmured its purpose as she slipped past, unintentionally whispering, "Optical Data Core." Before it could say more, al-D was gone in a burning flash of electronic intensity.

al-D didn't need the words to know where she was. Everything about the fiberlines screamed their purpose and intent. Bits of every image, every message, every surge of electricity that had ever flowed along the wire and glass and microfilament conduits were still there in some form or fashion. None of it was complete, but absorb enough of the bits, and she could extrapolate the bigger picture. A puzzle with half the pieces missing was still a recognizable image in the viewer's mind.

al-D filled in the missing pieces as she tripped, flashed, and surged down the lines of the Optical Data Core, her tiny fingers of electricity flashing out like miniature lightning bolts, touching, touching, touching, and absorbing anything she touched. After a short time—several nanoseconds, surely, which was a very long time for the Construct—completed images began forming in her cybernetic brain.

One scene (not her first, for hundreds and thousands were flooding her consciousness every nanosecond) flashed with the brilliance of a thousand sunrises. al-D recognized sunrises, although she had never seen one with real, true eyes. Other people had, and they had recorded their memories, and they had sent them along the fiberlines, and al-D now had their memories to share with her corporeal half when the darkness of nighttime took over, and they could be reunited once again. Now, though, a thousand sunrises flashed from the wires in a billion tiny bits of leftover bytes of information. It was the sun, Sol, Earth's primary, and the *Putin* was leaving her berth after her latest retrofit, gaining speed in a parabolic slingshot around the sun, flash, flash, flash, so hot, the skin of the ship burning, burning, burning, and al-D knew a moment of cybernetic jealously at the speed she had missed by not being there.

[[Hot! Hot! Must move faster!]]

She skirted along the wires, her electric fingertips of micro-lightning rolling, pulling, pushing her faster and faster. Images, many aboard the ship, flooded into her, and then, she reached a gold mine, a repository of optical data so vast she would have to cull and discard most of it before she fell back into the wires to continue her explorations.

She flipped through the images, hundreds, thousands, millions each nanosecond, so fast, so hot, so refreshing. Content, content, content, what's important, what's important? That's all that mattered to al-D. The images meant nothing to her, not as images to be admired or at which to be appalled. Many were beautiful, others indiscreet, all simply images, sets of digital bytes of information in specified patterns. al-D searched for specific patterns, what humans would call faces, involved in anything that would provide an advantage for General Agrippa's team on board the *Putin*. Who shook hands with whom, whispered in the dark with whom, gathered in out-of-the-way places with whom?

CASK

What alliances could be extrapolated from the images al-D sorted through? What motives could be painted across the assembled bytes of information? What crewmembers could be turned against the Captain to achieve Agrippa's nefarious ends?

[[Hot! Hot!]] In one cache, a hundred thousand images flashed through the Construct's lightning-electronic fingers, each one revealing some small facet of shipboard life, some saved, most shunted aside. Images of biometric data about the crew flashed through her fingertips, read in detail, and stored or shunted aside. Food preferences, revealed in charts and tables, hours slept, and with whom. It was all there, stored in optical databases, available for the Construct to peruse at her leisure.

Mere nanoseconds, and she had viewed them all. Third Mate Melnik holding paper images of Captain Devi, touching them with longing in her eyes. Navigator John in her quarters working on a math theorem in 3-D hologram format, one the Construct recognized as an unsolvable challenge that often absorbed the minds of the most brilliant mathematicians. A live feed of Technicians Hansen and Korhonen with Pilot-in-Command Mori playing a game with numbered wooden blocks. A shadowy image of First Helmsman Quispe and Second Helmsman Papadopoulos entwined in an intimate embrace, the background reflecting a crewman's quarters.

al-D paused for a nanosecond to sort the retained images into the most important and those of secondary importance, to make their absorption easier for her counterpart's slow meat-brain. Her human half was brilliant and carried engineered hardware to interface seamlessly with the Construct, but there were limits to meat-based computing power.

One image jumped out at her. Loadmaster Josiah Peeters, in the cargo hold, attempting to hide that he was entering information onto a Slideslip Drive. al-D flashed into extrapolation mode for a fraction of a nanosecond, compared cargo manifests, credit transfers, lists of missing materials, and came up with the logical conclusion.

Loadmaster Peeters was operating a black market for restricted goods. al-D's meat counterpart might find that very interesting, indeed.

al-D secured her images and flashed out of the lines leading to the Optical Data Core, the reverse trip through the gate seamless, as it only required permission going in one direction. Hot, hot, faster, faster, the Construct zipped along the lines, taking a turn leading to the propulsion systems of the massive starship. She could taste the faster-than-light drives, and they burned with the hot, hot fires of speed and intensity and unequaled levels of burning electricity. What information could she

CASK

absorb there?

Except! A wall! A gate! A hundred thousand electric stabs using her lightning fingers as keys, and it didn't respond! How frustrating!

[[Cold! Cold!]] al-D had paused too long. The fiberlines were absorbing her energy. She needed to move, move, move.

That was when she noticed she was being watched. That pause at the FTL gate was just enough to allow the Construct to sense that someone at some location in the ship was following her as she explored. She shrugged. It didn't matter. She could return at another time to the FTL aorta, the massive fiberline conduit that led directly into the propulsion systems. Her corporeal half could access the required permissions through the Uppernet. al-D would get in. She would get in.

[[Hot! Hot! Must keep moving. So much information to absorb!]]

—Chapter 21—

Interdicted Colony World *Verboten*

Ghost, Army Support Personnel
. . . who looks for trouble under each stone

"PYRO. OR DO YOU prefer Loki?"

I glanced sideways to catch the look on Pyro's green face. It struck me, surely Falco knew I'd hear every word. That meant his question was intended for me, not to answer, but to understand. His words had a double meaning, and I was intended to find the nuance among them. I recorded them on my suit's link and moved on. I'd have time to sort the subtleties later.

My skin crawled at what I carried in my hand, and in the hands of my comrades, as well. It was a shame the creature inside hadn't died in the crash. I had managed so far to keep my eyes from the fitful shape sleeping inside, lighted by the glow of the Cask's environmental programs. Unaided ears were deaf to what I could feel each step as I walked with the massive chest held in my hand.

The Cask had a heartbeat, the recurring thump signaling a beating muscle, the pressure of life's fluids circulating through connected veins, returning time and again to ensure life continued from moment to moment. Clicks and whirring traveled up my arm, little shivers that told of electrical neurons firing one after another, instructions given and received. The driving beat I felt wasn't from the creature, but from the Cask I carried. The pumps, delivery valves, plunger returns, and roller tappets working with mechanical precision, over and over, singing their song through my glove, spreading its music up my arm, and invading my skull, feeding into my inner ear, down my primary auditory cortex, and into my brain.

I wanted to wrap my hand into a fist and smash through the protective glass, quiet the noise that rang in my head, and be done with this violation to every moral principle I espoused as part of my dedication to defending Earth and her colonies.

I shifted my thoughts and reflected on my own internal systems. The Cask was heavy, ostentatiously the reason we accompanied the Envoy. Our suits' hydraulically powered exoskeletons were especially suited for it. We also had heartbeats, and not the ones in our chests, though we certainly had those. Miniature pumps assisted my ankles, my knees, my lower back, and my shoulders and arms.

My heart was all me. The Army hadn't yet figured a way to satisfactorily install a mechanical pump that was as durable and adjustable as the one humans were born with. No Iron Men for the modern Army. He was still a pipe dream, although I didn't doubt he was on someone's drawing board somewhere, ready to take our place when the last tests were run and the trials complete. Like the mythical Iron Man, with each step, my helmet displayed the pressure changes in each portion of my suit's hydraulics, with suction lines refilling the reservoirs, one-way valves grabbing the viscous fluid, compression springs clicking at every step, and pressure lines spurting fluid to make my mechanical joints stronger, stronger, stronger.

Being able to lift was more than starting and stopping. Momentum was momentum, and on Verboten, the gravity neared 1.4 Earth-normal, nearly that of Kepler 425b, the Envoy's world, more commonly referenced as Hanook. As we'd been heading downhill for the last kilometer, there'd been a real danger of falling, and Pyro, Recon, and I had coordinated our exoskeletons to improve traction on the increasingly muddy ground. Now that the ground had leveled, I released the link.

"Pyro, Recon, traction link released. You're on your own until we reach the city." Each man blinked acknowledgement in my helmet, the icon flashing green on my visor before fading away. I keyed just Pyro's audio. "What did you make of Falco's question?"

"Didn't see much in it, sir." He kept walking, with no other response.

"C'mon, man. I need feedback."

"I like the Doc, sir. His nickname is all right with me." Again, no additional response, but I should expect that from Pyro. He wasn't a verbal man. He liked to blow things up, not discuss why or how they should blow up. He had his strengths, if he could stay within his safe little world of explosive devices.

"I'm not asking about your love life. The elephant, man. The thing in the Cask. That's what Falco really asked about."

"Didn't read much in it, sir. He asked, and I answered. Even told him the truth, and that felt good."

"I bet it did." I looked at Pyro, his green-lighted faceplate aimed straight ahead, wondering what he was thinking. It was hard to tell with Pyro.

"Why do you ask, sir?"

That surprised me, coming from him. Maybe he had questions of his own and was just working them out. "Just thinking there was something else. Falco wouldn't ask something like that without a reason. You think he suspects anything?"

"Can't say, sir, and we've been careful. With

the ship down, don't think anyone's going to find anything. My reasoning, the Captain knows we're not fans of the thing in the box, so why'd we help? He knows Franklin, too, and everybody likes him. When he asked the question, I figured the truth would hold water better than any cock-up story I could devise."

"Good thinking, soldier. I expect you're right. Glad he asked you first. I might've said what I think."

"Yes, sir. Spect you would."

I looked over, about to make a crack back, and I caught a smile on his face. Not much, but it was there. I laughed, saying, "Yeah. I'll let Recon know we're sticking to your version."

I opened the channel for the three of us, to clue our third man in, although I suspected he was already on board. Pyro might be happy blowing things up, but Recon was a thinker. He noticed things, paid attention to them, and could extrapolate a whole battle scenario from a cracking branch under a man's boot. We had things under control. When the General arrived, he'd find all our ducks lined up, and our weapons hot and ready to fire. I was getting my promotion out of this. One way or another, this was my move up the ranks. If Pyro and Recon tagged along, I didn't mind. If they got in the way, like I said, this was my move up the ranks, one way or another.

CASK

Dreadnaught *Vladimir Vladimirovich Putin*

Operations Officer Ellery Martin
*. . . in which something surprising needs scrubbed
clean*

"WICKED THING THAT YOU ARE." Ops Officer Ellery Martin glared at the dialysis machine wedged into a niche in his quarters.

Shifting gears seamlessly, he tugged down the cuffs of his jacket and faced the door. With a thought, he pinged the opening mechanism and felt the subtle brush of the cabin's air displaced by the door as it disappeared into the wall with barely a sound.

A glint of paper packaging on the small desk caught his eye, and he caught himself before reacting. His arm tingled, just at the crook forming the inside of his elbow, although he recognized the tingling as psychosomatic. There had been no needle, simply a sharp push of air forcing the White

Ghost into his body, where it was quickly absorbed into his blood to be delivered to the cells in his brain.

He still waited, although he knew it wouldn't be long.

He had expected more time before being disturbed. Waiting? That hadn't been an option, nor was it an option now, although, of course, as the synthetic and highly illegal substance was already in his body, that cancelled out all the other options.

Now for the rush, the calming peace, the flood of generosity and well-being, and the focus that allowed him to perform his duties as the department head that ran the day-to-day operations of the team and interfaced between the CO and the rest of the ship.

Well, between Mission Commander Tesfaye and General Agrippa's team. It was a balancing act that was impossible, and Martin was expected to be on point and ready to handle any contingency at any time during the day.

He tried to focus. Who had pinged him? de Jong . . . no, Ali. Yes, the Commo, but no, that had been at the meeting with Agrippa. Ali had pinged them all, calling them to the meeting, and now Martin was in his quarters, recently juiced with White Ghost, but not yet feeling the supremely calming effect flood through his body.

CASK

And he had to carry on a civil conversation. It would strain every fabric of his drug-addicted brain.

An image of Loadmaster Peeters flashed in front of his eyes. Not real, not at the door, thank God. It was the White Ghost starting to filter into his brain, into his head, and into his thoughts. He had been unfocused with Peeters, demanding the man see him . . . *sell to him* immediately.

It was Martin's mind, his racing mind that forced him to ingest the White Ghost. That was all. He lived a lifetime every minute, caught up in every sensation, every image, every word spoken by himself or anyone else. He could tune nothing out, and he had watched Peeter's face, seen the muscles moving under the skin, the doubt, the greed, the irritation at the demand to provide the Ghost *now*. Then, Martin revealed his credits, and the man relaxed, his eyes cleared, and his lips formed a smile.

"Of course, Officer Martin. It's hard to live without Ghost, especially when you need it. Come. I believe I have enough to get you through a day or two."

A day or two! This ship. This ship! There had been no problem acquiring Ghost at home. And in some circumstances, it was legal, but not in the Army, and not on board the *Putin*. And certainly not for an officer of the fleet.

Thank God for Peeters, although the blessing came with its own curse. Now someone on the side of the enemy knew of Martin's flaw, and that didn't sit well with him even a small amount.

A small woman stepped to the door. Martin thought he might . . . *did* recognize her face, the fine features, the green eyes. His brain, thoughts rushing by. He hadn't been pinged. The message had come on the ship's comm. Work, Ghost. Get to it. Now's about time.

"Engineer Kazlauskas," she barked. She held a device in one hand that glowed with a pattern of lights, some brighter than others. It had a small screen for data entry. "Power generation and distribution. Do you have a minute, Officer Martin?"

"Certainly, Engineer." Martin kept his back rigid. Her first name came to him. Saskia. She was Third Engineer, under Apinelu, the one who carried a tablet and referenced it frequently. Not on the ship's Net, he had assessed, meaning Apinelu was on probation. This was her first mission, and if she didn't prove herself, this would likely be Apinelu's last.

"I have a power reading I would like to verify, if you don't mind." Kazlauskas smiled briefly, but she didn't salute or acknowledge his rank. A certain amount of residual hostility clouded the space between them, something continually present between the ship's crew and the Army team that had infringed on their domain.

Martin felt his mind clearing as the world around him slowed down. It was the Ghost enabling him to tamp down the sensory input flooding his brain. Thank God for Ghost, he breathed.

"Power reading?" The Ghost flowed downward, and Martin's arms released their locked position. He motioned around the room in a fluid gesture. "Quarters are quarters. What could be creating an abnormal power reading in here?" He smiled, and he was pleased to feel the expression move across his face in a natural and timely way. He was in control when he had White Ghost on his side.

"Tools, scanners, an unregistered exoskeleton?" She chuckled at that, keeping her eyes on him as she stepped inside. The door slipped closed behind her.

"An exoskeleton?" He moved his arms disjointedly and comically. The Ghost was starting to feel good. "What for?"

"Sorry. Just came from the Stasis Barracks. It seems your team brought about three hundred on board that no one warned us about. The power grid has been stressed trying to balance out the energy draw, and I've spent the last half day readjusting flow meters."

"Okay." Martin knew about the exoskeletons,

one for each of the clones in the barracks. He'd suggested they be precharged, but al-Din had overridden him. Said they would be easier to load—meaning easier to load in secret—if their power cells were discharged.

"Now they have me checking all power anomalies with your team, and one of them is in this room. No exoskeleton, so, any ideas?" She tapped her screen, but she didn't lower the device.

"Engineer Kazlauskas, may I call you Saskia?" The White Ghost was in full effect, and Martin felt his confidence surge. He was the Operations Officer, and he was good at what he did, and personable, too. He also remembered something Peeters had let slip during their first conversation about a relationship the Engineer had enjoyed with the Chief Officer of the Deck.

"You know my name?" The Engineer seemed surprised.

"Of course. How are you and Officer Jónsdóttir these days?" He smiled warmly.

"Ulric? How do you—" Her face reddened, and she let the hand with the device fall to her side.

"Come now, Saskia. Isn't it obvious? You two are made for one another. Did something happen between you?" He motioned to a built-in divan, and she melted into it. He sat beside her and took her hand.

"I . . . I—" She looked at him, and her eyes

were red.

"What is it? It's just me, and what you say stays with me. We're only on board for this one mission, and you'll never see us again. By us, I mean me. You can trust me." Wouldn't the General be pleased if this were something they could use?

"I . . . you're right. There was something there, and the first time, it was good. I thought Ulric might be a shortcut out of Engineering. But Ulric is a ladies' man, always that, and he was off to a new conquest before I knew what had happened." She laughed softly and drew her hand away. "The second time didn't end so easily. I demanded monogamy, and that was the end of that."

She covered her face and looked away, and Martin said, "But you still care." He glanced at the dialysis machine in its niche. Now to keep her distracted until he could get her out the door.

"If it would get me out of engineering." She forced a bright expression on her face, making it clear she wanted to move past the subject. "So, Officer Martin, no exoskeletons, so I can clear your quarters." She lifted her device and tapped the screen, which turned it green for a moment before the color melted into a neutral gray, and she stood. "Thank you for your time."

Martin watched her leave with a brisk step, and when the door closed after her, he took a deep breath, looked hard at the dialysis machine, and he felt it mocking his feelings of calm and confidence, as if it wanted to strip it all away.

And it would, tonight while he slept. It would scrub his blood clean. It was the way it had to be, unless he wanted to claim augmented brain-enhancement wetware glitches, and no one would believe that. It was a hypothetical but impractical application of military hardware, and he wasn't sure anyone would believe the Army had been foolish enough to try it out on him.

—Chapter 23—

Interdicted Colony World *Verboten*

Medical Officer Richard Franklin
. . . who plays a game of bumper cars

I KEPT ALERT FOR SIGNS of injuries in our party. I had eleven people to keep track of, or to be literal, nine people, one Cygnian Envoy, and an Android that could shift guises to become whatever he needed to be for the moment, even a medical surgery assist unit. Still, he occasionally required care, and that's the job I'd been assigned.

I pulled my glass from my belt and checked my latest status reports. What I expected to see was a complete diagnostic from the Cask, which should be updating in real time. I ran down the display, tapping an icon, to see the display wink, and a list of information slide onto the screen. Battery levels were holding true to expectations, and communication links showed a strong signal, although no messages had come through; the movement across the rough ground hadn't seemed to impact the Envoy in any meaningful negative way. In other words, the diplomat was fine. I moved to the main display and touched Jollenbeck's icon. Coming down the hillside, Ssanyu and I had wrestled with Cryp's chair, repeatedly encouraging him that our arms and legs were more easily recharged than his batteries. Let us do the work. The boy finally joined us, and on the smoother terrain, he and the Android put their shoulders to work, for which both I and Toofer were expressly grateful.

I glanced at my glass, taking in the Science Officer's current status, and was surprised to see a message icon blinking. I looked at him, in conversation with the Acolyte, his Aakash blinking away, and back to my glass. I'm with him, at his side, ready to talk when he needs, I thought, so the message means something. These were words he wanted no one else to hear. I tapped the icon and began to read.

—Medical Officer Franklin, I don't wish to impose, but I have concerns; and with the ship offline for the foreseeable future, I have no choice but to depend on your eyes and ears.

—As we were landing, I managed to procure a Data Dump, not all of which I've had opportunity to access thoroughly. However, transmissions at the time of our crash suggested no life signs on Verboten. So, our first objective should be reaching a communications center. Daimler-Porsche should have a primary hub set up in the city center. If our early reports are validated, Daimler-Porsche will send rescue faster than anyone else, because it's in their best financial interest. Two other things. The Envoy was transmitting a message and interrupted. With the tension between the Army and the Cygnians, I hope our current situation isn't an escalation of tensions already strung too tight. Also, check atmospherics for toxins. Your input will be invaluable—

I clicked, Message Read, and watched it shoot off the edge of my display. The rest of Jollenbeck's indicators seemed acceptable, considering we were off the ship, and he was working off battery reserves. I tried to pull up his Tesla reactor, and it gave me an error message, worrisome in the long run, but not a problem for the time being. My atmospheric sensors were offline without the ship, so I shrugged that off.

Backing out, I wasn't surprised to see that I was blocked from accessing the Army's three soldiers. My icons indicated they were either green or not. Green, I was told, meant they were alive—which I'd have to be blind not to see, as they were carrying the Envoy—and red would paint them dead. The rest was restricted on a need-to-know basis. I guess they thought I didn't need to know and had locked me out. I shrugged. I was aware of the tension between the soldiers and the others on this trip. I liked the three men well enough, despite it all, and I could do nothing about the opinions of others. If they wanted to bump heads, I had to leave it at that.

As we neared the city, the grass fell away, getting shorter, or perhaps being trimmed tighter, it was hard to tell. It didn't look like it'd been trimmed recently. Perhaps Jollenbeck's message was correct, the city was vacated. If so, it didn't make sense. Cryp was right, saying that Daimler-Porsche was a powerful enterprise, and they'd laid a claim to Verboten. They wouldn't tolerate intrusion into their territory, and the people? Someone had to run the mining and exploratory expeditions. At the least, Daimler's people should be here to oversee the corporation's rights and property. They wouldn't want it to be lost.

"Doctor, what'cha thinking?" We'd stopped for a rest, and Song was sipping water from a metal canteen. "All this, no people? It's odd, in my book."

"As in mine." I was checking my glass regularly, and the Android's icon was blinking. "Excuse me," I murmured, pulling it free from my belt and tapping it. I must have let the news write itself on my face, because Song questioned me about it.

"A message? Not good?" Song capped her

canteen and slipped it into its holder. She was right to ask. As First Mate, she outranked me, and my information was valuable to her. Anything shared with Song could potentially benefit our team.

"Little is, today." I let my eyes rove those with us, the three soldiers sitting on a reproduction stone wall, still encased in their artificial skins and bristling with armor. The wall was clearly fake, because it was broken in one place, and underneath the exterior, the damage exposed a rough concrete structure. The Envoy rested some distance from them, as if they might be contaminated if they remained nearby. The Acolyte had rejoined the Bishop since we'd reached flatter ground. The Boss was with Ssanyu and having a quite spirited conversation with Jollenbeck. Green flashed across his Aakash repeatedly, revealing the nature of their interaction. Jokes were being shared, no doubt salty ones, with those involved.

"What do you remember of Verboten, First Mate?" I smiled at her, hoping she'd answer me without questioning my motives too stridently.

"We're here, so trees, green grass, and a beautiful city, if one that's shy on people." She smiled back.

"Clearly. We can touch it all, so it must be true. But what do you remember? Recall the treaty with Daimler-Porsche. What did they want here?"

"Sure, I'll give it a shot. This planet has heavy

metals, mainly iridium, palladium, and chromium. Oh," she snapped her fingers, "astatine, and lots of it, found naturally nowhere else."

"So, where are the mines?" I smiled and motioned around me. It was green as far as we could see.

"Underground, I'd say."

"Certainly possible, but unlikely. On an undeveloped world, plentiful resources are widely available at surface level, or just below the surface. That's how they're discovered. Strip mining is the most profitable method of removal." I glanced at my glass again, checking on the Android to make sure I hadn't misread his data.

"The Android, still?" Song pointed to my glass. When I gave her a puzzled look, she tapped her temple. "There's a reason I'm First Mate. Just because the ship's down doesn't mean my brain is."

"You've been keeping tabs on our soldiers?" I nodded that way with a grin.

"Maybe. Tell me about the Android." She moved closer, although she didn't try to look too closely. Number 2 is like that, sharp but considerate. I liked her and enjoyed working with her.

"I'm reading an anomaly in its diagnostics." I tapped the glass. I still hadn't figured it out, and the Acolyte had developed a cough. That bothered me.

"Anything I can help with?"

CASK

Across from us, the soldiers had gathered at the Cask again, preparing to move on. I shook my head, motioning. "I suppose we're moving." My glass dinged, and I checked it, to see a message from Jollenbeck.

—We're headed into the city. The Army's already on the move. Join us if you have time, Medical Officer Franklin. I'd enjoy visiting with you about our little unfinished lab experiment—

"It's official," I said, acknowledging his request. "Our Science Officer has asked me to join him. Do you mind?"

The Bishop's Acolyte had joined us, and I nodded to him to speak. He stifled a cough, and I noticed red eyes. I remembered Jollenbeck's toxins. I ignored a tickle in my own throat and hoped it was nothing.

"Officer Song, His Holiness wishes to have a word with you, if you can spare the time."

"Perfect timing, Doctor." She winked at me and turned to the boy, asking, "I noticed you were helping out our Science Officer. Did Officer Jollenbeck tell you any amusing stories . . ."

A pleasant and well-adjusted woman all around, able to converse with youths and handle a weapon at the same time. I'm sure she has tricks up her sleeve only she knows about.

I took my time getting to Jollenbeck. He could message me if he had insights he thought especially witty or vital. We were entering the city, and I was interested in the architectural aspects of the place. I was certain the Army men would be observing tactical objectives, like the tower at the entrance where the grass turned firmly to a paved surface. It was glassed at the top, with an overhanging roofline. Decorative, I supposed, as it revealed no openings for firing weapons. What would our soldiers see, a guard post, motion-tracking cameras, or an early warning system for the populace sequestered deeper in the city's core? Another direction, a spire thrust into the sky, possibly a religious edifice. On worlds everywhere, it was a standard building theme. It was as if gods were always in the heavens above whatever world one happened to live on. It seemed to me it would be more convenient for the people who worshipped in the edifices if their gods lived among them. Then they would know the trials and tribulations their subjects endured and understand better how to serve them.

Song had made it to the Bishop. She waved as I watched, and I returned it. They were passing a dry fountain, one with a decorative serpent twisting into the air, quite beautiful, possibly brass or gold leaf. Song pointed to it, probably seeing the beauty in the unusual. The Acolyte looked the direction she pointed, and the Bishop intentionally looked away. I wanted to laugh. A red apple gleamed, suspended just out of the serpent's mouth, and I pictured the cathedral I thought I'd seen. Was the fountain a symbol of frustrated desire? Both pointed to the skies, perhaps pleading for help, one for redemption, and the other for forbidden pleasure. I saw no difference in this world—separated from the rest of the galaxy for over a hundred years—and the rest of mankind, stumbling over each other in confusion. The answer to man's problems was always what one didn't have, be it in the sky or on the ground at our feet.

"Captain," I called, finally close enough to Falco, Jollenbeck, and Ssanyu to make my entreaty a casual one, as though I happened to be near to them.

"Franklin! Are we having an adventure?" He raised his hand and pointed. I looked up to a tower thrusting even higher than the cathedral spire. "That's our destination. Our excellent Science Officer's been sharing his viewpoints, and I agree. We're conserving his power, although Aldrik doesn't appreciate our generous help. However, I'm Captain, and that trumps even the old cryp's loud voice, wouldn't you say?" He smiled as he patted Jollenbeck on the shoulder, even though he wouldn't be able to feel it. "Would you like to have a push?"

"Even more, I'd enjoy spending time with my friend. Here in the city, I can manage alone.

Toofer, if you wish to explore with the Captain—"
I shrugged, indicating I had no strong opinion
either way. I caught the change in Ssanyu's personality. Her eyes dropped, and she reached and
placed a hand on the Science Officer's cheek,
pausing just for a moment. "You are among more
than coworkers. We are your friends. Remember
that always, my lovely man." Then her arm fell, her
eyes narrowed, and she called, "I'm missing the
Android. Captain, have you seen him?"

As they left in search of our missing
compatriot, I smiled. We were stranded on an
unusual world, one that wasn't anything like we'd
been led to believe, and it was wonderful. The
people I shared my day with, no matter who it
happened to be, filled me with pleasure. Even our
Army soldiers, with their gruff natures and skewed
loyalties, were gems of diversity that made each
moment sparkle brighter than the one before.

We were passing the cathedral, and a massive
statue was affixed over the front doors. It took me
by surprise. It was a dead man being held by a
weeping woman. I would have expected a round-
bellied Buddha, a many-armed Kali, or a winged
Michael of Christendom, something to portray love
or power, not a symbol of death.

Even when the sight of the dead man was long
past us, something kept it fixed in my mind, as
though it was a warning I shouldn't ignore.

CASK

—Chapter 24—

Dreadnaught *Vladimir Vladimirovich Putin*

Communications Officer Garian Ali
. . . who finds electricity and water mix very well

COMMO GARIAN ALI let the saline water bath wash his skin. The hardware threaded through his body, forming oversized veins down his arms and legs, warmed as the link nodules at his joints glowed.

Ali was shunted, and he could taste his filfel as it permeated the Uppernet, the powdered peppers and crushed garlic everyone teased him about boasting *Ali* in each probe, each interrogation, the acrid bark of his presence sublimated only when he desired anonymity or secrecy. It was the taste of revenge to Ali, a carved dagger of bitter herbs and spices, one that would soon be felt by the enemy they had come to destroy.

Ali had tailed al-Din's Construct, faster and more efficiently than the narrowly focused electronic device. Each door it had opened, Ali had also slipped through, piggybacked, released to cover more ground than the little Construct could.

Understanding was what gave Ali his advantage. The al-Din Construct could gather, and gather it did, but to make sense of, to apply intuition, to *think*, that took a human brain.

Not like Müller. Ali knew the Traino was a drone, although Müller's operators had been very thorough. Nah, nothing got past Ali, not even the bomb in Müller's head. Ali understood the reason for it, but it wasn't necessary. He—*Ali*—was the trump card on this mission. Even General Agrippa knew how important, how *vital,* Ali was. Sure, he'd lost contact with Hernandez, McAvoy, and Nissen, but they'd lost contact with the whole freakin' ship. Then, that was Hernandez, McAvoy, and Nissen's job, wasn't it? Take care of the Cask and that monstrosity from Cygnus.

The taste of filfel burned back through Ali's feed, choking him with the acrid peppers and garlic. It was good, though, his Libyan heritage burning the oppressors that had once tried to enslave his people.

He pictured the Italian boot, and his anger boiled. Around him, the saline solution steamed, bubbles rising as the water was forced from its liquid phase into gaseous pockets of air as the water was pushed beyond its ability to retain the molecules in their liquid form.

Ali linked to the cooling pumps, sending them a message through the Uppernet to increase the waterflow, and he sensed the heightened movement of the water around him, as the super-heated liquid was vacuumed away into the transparent piping surrounding his water bath; and he felt cooled saline solution flooding around him.

Seamlessly, with little more than a tiny fragment of his mental processing power, the Commo pinged General Agrippa.

"General, Commo Ali here. Found what you're looking for. Other news, I'm stitching together a crew quilt that you can unravel at your convenience, sir. Details at your ready. Ali out."

Captain Devi wouldn't sense his brazen message, nor would Commanding Officer Tesfaye. Ali ruled the Uppernet, he and his team. The Commo had dipped his electronic fingers into enough crew pie to taste the undercurrents of who might be turned and who would stick by Captain Devi when General Agrippa made his move. The *Putin* and her crew were no more than imperialist minions of the Great Satan, unable to do more than shovel hot dogs and junky down the world's resources.

Tesfaye was on Agrippa's team in principle, but it was a tossup whom the Commander would side with when the moment of decision came.

Pilot-in-Command Mori. They needed him, though he wasn't in with them yet. Still, Ali now had the goods on Technician Korhonen. Perhaps he hadn't agreed to become a sieve bleeding information to the terrorists on Earth, but the suggestion that he could be tagged as subversive . . . Ali was confident he would fold, and he'd picked up on Mori's desperate need for approval from his cabinmates. Pull Korhonen in, and he and Hansen—a cousin, perfect!—would break with Devi. They were the key to Mori's acceptance of the new command when it happened.

Ali felt good about Mori. Really good.

Ali was also confident that Peeters was theirs. Ops Martin thought his addiction (there wasn't much Ali didn't know) was his weakness, but it was a strength that would swing Peeters to the winning side. It was a plus that the black marketeer controlled ship's stores. Two wins in Ali's book.

Quispe and Papadopoulos were important to Devi, though there was contention in the mix. Ali was still working on how to get the most out of that.

Chief Rodriguez? Ali accepted he would side with Devi. He might have to be taken out, although the Commo hated the idea of eliminating an officer of the line. It went against the grain of everything the Army stood for, even if it might be necessary. Ali hoped to find another alternative, but with time down to the wire, that might not be possible.

Flight Officer Melnik. The Commo had put her in a priority category early on. The woman was clearly infatuated with the Captain, but she also felt a level of revulsion at her Indian background. General Agrippa had concurred this was useful information and to keep it forefront in their plans.

Through very recent Uppernet eavesdropping on Martin and Engineer Kazlauskas, Ali knew the Engineer could be encouraged—twisted—into cutting Jónsdóttir at the knees. A promise of a promotion, and she was theirs.

Ali's net connection pinged, and he effortlessly shifted his list to another set of synapses in his brain, and he connected to the Net.

"Yah, Ali here."

"Agrippa. Make it good, Commo. I need good news, and I need it fast."

"Yessir." Ali clicked his systems into high gear, and the saline around him bubbled with an excess output of heat before the pumps could ramp up. He grew warm for a moment before he felt the water begin to cool. "I've received a location ping for the *Roosevelt*—"

"About time! Tell me where, and I'll get this bucket on the way before another watch comes on duty."

"Yeah, hold up, General. That's going to be a problem." Ali sucked in a deep breath and held it.

"Spit it out, Commo." The growl bled through

over the Uppernet.

"A ping's all I got, and I think I know why."

"Let me line this up. First, you say you have a location, and now you say you don't. That's not like you, Ali. You're better than this. So, what are you not saying?"

"I suspect, and that's all I can do, General, because there's nothing out there any longer, but I suspect the *Roosevelt* may have gone aground."

"Aground. An Interstellar Ranger. And Falco's good, too good to let his ship run aground. He may be not military, but he could have been." Agrippa's terse observation steamed over the Net, demanding clarification. How could what's not possible have happened now and in this disastrous situation?

"Hernandez, sir." Ali waited on that one, hoping the General would put it together without his help.

"Hernandez. He replaced Müller, I recall. And that means? Connect it for me, Commo."

"This is a longer story, General, and I have to give you all of it. You know Müller was scheduled to head the team on the *Roosevelt*. So, what happened? Why the swap? Here's what you don't know. Müller is a bomb waiting to go off."

"Hell, son, everyone on this ship knows that. What's your point?"

"No, sir, you don't understand." Ali was being careful, watching his language, and doing this by the book. He didn't need this to bleed back on him. "A real bomb, in his head. That's why he didn't make it onto the *Roosevelt*. His operating systems weren't fully approved by FusionTech. He wasn't a hundred percent integrated and wasn't released by his team."

"FusionTech. You mean the man's a . . . I can hardly say it. I have a *robotic drone* on my team? If that doesn't beat all. And he has a *what* in his head? A bomb?"

"Sir, now you understand Hernandez and what I suspect happened to the *Roosevelt*. He must have sent out a locater buoy for us when he decided to take the ship down. That's what pinged us. The only thing that could take down the locator buoy would be—"

"A massive magnetic field just like the one around Verboten. Commo, that's not good news. This ship can handle it, right?"

"Yessir. Don't think Devi's going to want to go there, though. The place is proscribed."

"We'll see about that. You say Müller's got a bomb in his head? He must have multiple operators quantum linked to his operational systems. Do they know you have their number?"

"No, sir."

"And you can hijack Müller?"

"I expected you'd ask, and yes, without a question." Ali smiled, and he relaxed in his watery bath, letting the pumps slow to a trickle.

"That's our backup plan. You didn't find out if any of my men survived on that godforsaken world, did you?"

"Sorry, sir."

"Thought not. Be that as it may, I need control of this ship. What about the crew? Who can we count on?"

"I've got a list in the works. And we've got three hundred drones with powered-up exoskeletons in the Stasis Barracks. I can defrost them in under an hour."

"Not so fast, cowboy." Even over the Uppernet, Ali could hear the General take a breath. "This will be easier if I have Tesfaye on my side. Let me see where he stands before I make my move."

"If you say so, sir."

"Verboten, you say. That's a crock. Agrippa out."

If the Uppernet could fizzle—and that was impossible—it popped and burned with miniature electric firecrackers, reverberating with the General's forceful signoff. Here was the thing. Ali hadn't said. Not the planet, and he certainly hadn't identified Verboten, although there was no other viable alternative.

The Commo sent a request to Flight Officer Sharipov—on loan from the Navy—for a tentative course to Verboten. She was the back-seat mission commander, and a request from her wouldn't involve the Putin's crew. Even so, he kept his request neutral, as the Flight Officer didn't have access to the team's Uppernet, and he didn't need this making the crew's gossip rounds before their destination was firmed up.

"Commo Ali to Officer Sharipov. Requesting a hypothetical course change to intersect with the interdicted planet Verboten. Off the record, please. This is a private enquiry for personal reasons."

Might as well be prepared, Ali thought, shifting back to his personnel quilt. He recalled a video feed from the Mess. Sharipov had seemed highly attracted to Chief Officer Jónsdóttir. He thought that might be a play to sway the man's allegiance to their side. Jónsdóttir was exceptionally well thought of by the crew, and if he could be brought on board, the rest might be a piece of cake.

Except for Rodriguez, but that wasn't something Ali wanted to think about just then.

—Chapter 25—

Interdicted Colony World *Verboten*

Pyro, Army Support Personnel
. . . for whom itchy fingers are a means to an end

NIKOLAUS SHERRELL NISSEN.

Is it any wonder I blow things up? Sherrell. What were my parents thinking?

And Ghost. *Pyro, or do you prefer Loki.* What's the reason for asking me that? Do I have to prefer one over the other?

Except I do. Only because I like Franklin, and it is his name for me. Loki, like the Norse god. Plucky, in and out, and lots of fire.

That's me! Lots of fire, things blowing up, things going boom. I like being Loki.

This thing I'm carrying, though, that's different. I'm helping transport it because Franklin asked, that's the only reason.

Too bad Müller's not here. He was our plan, get to the Cask, set himself off, and Recon and I could limp back home on the *Roosevelt.* Then Ghost showed up, said plans were changed, and we had to do this differently.

I wanted to blow up the Cask. Nah, Ghost said. Might come back on the Army, reflect on the General. We had to find another way.

So, Ghost had me sabotage the *F.D.R.* You're welcome, Captain. Your lowly lieutenant did your dirty work, and now look at us.

I glanced up at the sky, wondering when the General would find us. If he would find us. Who could have predicted the ship would divert to Verboten, of all places? Well, not a problem, not if the ship had been military-spec. They hadn't considered the *Roosevelt*'s ARDs couldn't compensate for Verboten's extreme conditions.

How I would have loved to be on the outside watching the *Roosevelt* tear through the atmosphere, the flames leaping from her superstructure as she was compromised, the trees along the ridge grasping at the old girl, shredding her underbelly as she stumbled and split open, spilling her guts along a kilometer-long trench of devastation and destruction.

Pyro's fingers squeezed the handle on the Cask tighter. They itched inside his suit.

Burn, baby, burn, he sent mentally to the creature he couldn't see in its mechanical box.

For you, General. Burn, baby, burn.

—Chapter 26—

Dreadnaught *Vladimir Vladimirovich Putin*

Captain Kalinda Devi
. . . takes a spill off a wild roller coaster ride

THE GOOD CAPTAIN was dealing with a moment of doubt, something very unusual to her.

Normally—as in every day since graduating the Academy some decade-and-a-half earlier—Devi had known a sense of purpose and direction that was uncanny. Well, uncanny to anyone who was not Kalinda Devi. To Devi, it was as natural as breathing. She knew from experience not everyone was as driven with faith in their actions as she was, which was why she demanded unqualified cooperation with her plans and decisions.

Opinions? Of no account if they did not line up with Devi's.

Now, though, with Agrippa and his team aboard her ship, and the trial of dealing with the Mission Commander as an intermediary between her Navy crew and Agrippa's vile sense of self-satisfied entitlement and bigotry, something ate at her.

Devi stepped to a thick, reinforced glass panel opening to the depths of space. She palmed a smaller panel at its side, and outside of the *Putin*, a thick section of the ship's hull withdrew. Through the glass, she took in the blackness. She was unsure why the designers installed these massively useless openings in the hulls of the Navy's ships. There was nothing out there. Oh, near a planet, she could sometimes catch a glimpse of something interesting, but it was a return of inconsequential value compared to the structural rigidity it negated in the hull.

And traveling at superlight speeds. Not even the stars were visible. The *Putin* outran the light of every star in the galaxy. A red tinge at the edges of the thick glass reminded her that there was light out there, just not any that was visible to human eyes. The ship skimmed the envelope of known space, touching too lightly to allow something so simple as starlight to step up and say hello.

Devi turned, and as the window acknowledged the lack of her attention, the section of hull that had so recently shifted aside moved once more—silent through the thick, insulating exterior skin of the spaceship—and closed off the blackness of space from the brightly lighted interior of the Captain's quarters.

A dainty pot steamed on a console. It shared the space with a small lamp, a figurine with many arms in a commanding pose, and a fragile cup. The Captain lifted the pot and drew in a deep, satisfied breath as the clear amber liquid sluiced from the spout of the pot and curled deliciously in the cup.

"One good thing the British gave my people," she murmured, as she lifted the cup and let its humid warmth wash her face.

She carried the cup carefully to her desk as she mulled over her doubts—not quite worries, but very close—about this entire mission. She had known from the onset that Agrippa would buck her authority on board the *Putin*. The virulence of his insistence on that Ali creature with its liquid-cooled shunt system tied into the ship's communication grid . . . an entire cabin had to be converted for the series of pumps and cooling units for the IT officer's saline bath. A waste, an unholy waste, but what was she to do? She was only the Captain of the ship that had been appropriated to move Agrippa's team all this distance into the void of space.

And for what? To support a diplomatic mission that already carried three of the Army's best trained hotshots. And they weren't anywhere near the battle zones where the real fighting was happening.

It didn't make any sort of sense, like three

hundred clones with fully charged exoskeletons. Devi wondered if Agrippa thought she'd missed that. She was fully aware they were transported on board with the exoskeletons' battery banks drained, and that they had been taxing the ship's electrical grid for days as they rebuilt their power reserves. For what purpose? She had enough firepower on the *Putin* to wipe out most of a planet's surface, if things came to that, though she expected it never would. She could hardly see the use of the clones. Who was there to fight in this segment of the galaxy, at least that would require physical augmentation on the ground?

She was certain the Cygnian Envoy played a bigger part in this charade than anyone let on. Whatever Agrippa had in mind, she was determined she was the one to thwart his plan. The *Putin* was under her command, and that was just the way it was.

Devi lifted her cup, held it with the tips of the fingers on both hands, and decided it had cooled enough for her to risk a sip. Just as it touched her lips, the comm panel on her desk dinged. She paused, waiting. Murphy had the helm. Any official enquiries would be directed to the Bridge. This was a direct connection, self-powered and independent of the rest of the vessel. She could imagine no reason for being interrupted on this line while in her private quarters.

"Murphy to Devi. Urgent, ma'am. Please respond if you can." He yelled something, but his voice cut off before she could tell what it was.

If she could concerned her, but not as much as the background noises the First Mate's microphone had picked up. Devi replaced her cup on her desk, much faster than she had lifted it, and she keyed the comm.

"Captain to the Bridge. Murphy?" She released the switch, only to have the unit blare its response.

"Mutiny, ma'am. Best you stay there till this is under control. Can you override Communications from there? I've tried, but the Bridge has been hijacked. We've got nothing here. Even the doors are frozen."

"Who—" Agrippa wouldn't dare! Someone had, however. She could hear the efforts to break out of the Bridge—people yelling, and what must be chairs slamming against the lift doors.

"That Müller chap. Off his rocker, ma'am. Sorry, that's harsh, but it's true. It's like there's not a human in that body. He's hijacked by a devil, skewering anyone that gets in his way. Any help you can give us from there. Anything, ma'am."

"Will give it a try."

"Thank you, ma'am. Murphy out."

Devi found she was holding her prayer cloth between two fingers. She didn't remember withdrawing it from her sleeve. If the Bridge were compromised, she didn't expect she would have any success from here. She pulled up a screen and keyboard, searching for video feeds that might tell her what was taking place. At first, she was locked out of everything, but she knew passwords and overrides that were hers and hers alone. She was the Captain, and she knew this ship better than any interlopers could. After some moments of intense frustration, she located a series of hardline video feeds left undisturbed from a long-ago refit, and she attempted a password she thought she'd forgotten from many years before.

"Blessings, Mata Vaishnodevi," Devi whispered, as a gridwork of video feeds flickered on, covering her screen.

Her blood chilled at what she saw, and she felt her eyes water at the humiliation. In scene after scene, her crew, many dirtied or bloodied. At opened doors, blank-faced men swathed in exoskeletons, many battle-scarred, held weapons in their hands. The faces of the men glowed as if freshly awakened, and Devi was sure they were. Clones all, swarming her ship in their brutal battle armor. Several doors were crushed, as if they had been forced open by the exoskeleton-clad soldier drones. On more than one, streaks of red told of her crew defending their ground.

Devi scrolled through the video feeds. Not all the ship was available on this outdated system.

That shunted freak, she said to herself, before clamping down on her thoughts. Even in this disaster, she would not allow such harsh condemnations in her head. Yet, it angered her, for it must be Communications Officer Ali responsible for this. No one else had access. Devi had told them, she had *told them,* and they had refused to listen. She had told them what she would do, and they had ignored her pleas to keep that creature off her ship.

There. The Medical Bay. Devi enlarged the image. It was from a poor angle, the old camera now partially obscured behind a storage cabinet. She could just see Jónsdóttir, as he removed his shirt to expose a bloodied arm. He turned, and Devi shuddered at a gash from his collarbone up beside one ear. An arm she didn't recognize pressed clean gauze against the wound.

"Good," Devi whispered. "I hope someone paid. Thank you, Ulric. You've made me proud."

Other scenes revealed crew members huddled on bunks—Quispe and Papadopoulos in one feed—and several in the Mess, their distraught faces answering the questions Devi couldn't ask. She scanned the faces, relieved to find Hansen and Korhonen, shoulder to shoulder. They were speaking privately to one another with intensity. They appeared unharmed, and Devi felt a small measure of relief flood her. There were glimpses of Agrippa's team, but Devi's eyes were for her crew.

She'd hoped this feed would give her access to the Bridge, but she expected not, and such was the case. The video feeds from there were in the new system only, updated in the refit and unavailable to her.

Murphy, she pleaded silently. Do nothing rash. Survive to take our ship back from the interlopers.

One image especially distressed her, though not as much as she might have expected. Mission Commander Tesfaye. It seemed he had tried to control the General . . . and failed. She found him slumped over in a corridor feed, limp with the side of his face blackened.

Her comm dinged. She turned to it in dread. Even so, she engaged it. "Devi here."

"Murphy, ma'am. Are you okay?"

"As okay as I can be." She released an involuntary breath. "I have video feeds across the ship. Is the Bridge still ours?"

"No, ma'am. Nothing is. They are coming in. I expect they'll come for you next. I've tried to emergency seal your quarters. Hope my signal got through. Take—"

His transmission cut off when a voice yelled, "You! With the red hair. Get off that comm!" The comm hissed and immediately dinged again as though a second transmission had been waiting for Murphy's interrupted signal.

"Murphy?" Devi hoped desperately.

"Rodriguez, Captain." The sounds of fighting nearly obscured his urgent whisper. "It's that Müller. They claim he's got a bomb in his head. He's a drone, Captain, and he doesn't care who he kills. This is a screwup all around. I'll hold Engineering while I can. No! It's another of those damned exoskeletons breaking through the door." He yelled, "Not now, you traitorous hunk of metal—"

The comm chirped and the sound died. Devi looked at her cup of tea. It still steamed, and she lifted it and took a small sip. Warm, but no longer hot. *Ah, as well. I cannot enjoy it now, anyway.*

Thumping noises fed through her door, and she stood, pulled gently at the cuffs of her sleeves, and moved to the front of her desk. She flinched as the door was forced open. She wished she had time to access her personal weapons. She had fight left in her if they gave her an opportunity. That's all she asked for, an opportunity.

First through the damaged door was one of the blank-eyed, fresh-skinned clones. His heavy exoskeleton whirred and clanked as he took up a position to the side, and a second soldier came through, matching him on the opposite side of the door. Then, in marched Training Officer Kasem Müller, taking a position with his hands behind his back. His eyes locked on her with disregard for her position of authority as Captain on board the *Putin*.

CASK

In stepped General Agrippa, his face of folded leather polished against his stony eyes. He appeared carved from granite and obsidian. At his side were his Pilot-in-Command Kaua'i Mori and the beautiful Jelena Sharipov. Second Engineer Lilou Apinelu accompanied them, her eyes downcast. Devi looked for restraints on the *Putin* engineer. There were none.

"General." Devi spoke first. "Next?"

"I like you," the General barked, with an unexpected laugh. "Maybe not like, but I'll give you respect. We just took your ship, and you only have one word for me. That's good."

"My Second Engineer. What do you require of her?" Devi's blood felt as hot as the Indian sun. Surely, surely Apinelu didn't stand with these people of her own accord. It was not possible!

"Captain, you misunderstand the situation. It's not what I want from her. It's what she wants from us. Off your ship." Agrippa reached into a pocket and pulled out a cigar. The brown paper was banded with a logo that promised smoke-free enjoyment. He bit the end off and spat it on the floor. Sucking hard on the cigar, the end flared, and it began to glow. He puffed it several times, breathing deep and relishing the moment.

"And next?'

"I own your ship, Captain—"

"You own nothing, General. This ship is mine,

and I will have control of it."

"Someday, maybe, when I've found my men. For now, though, it's mine, easy or hard. You can encourage your crew to aid us, or we can fly this ship without them. I have Naval Flight Officer Sharipov for that, and I'm sure we won't do too much damage to the propulsion system, now that the good Second Engineer is with us." Agrippa chuckled. "Oh, and your First Engineer isn't happy. I'm getting reports that he's been cuffed and locked in his quarters. I've got a soldier in with him to make sure he doesn't try any fancy moves."

"Rodriguez? You . . . I was just on the comm with him. How can you . . ." She had seen no one give him a report on her Chief Officer of Engineering.

"Yeah, you didn't know we can do that. There's lots about us you don't know. Easy or hard, your choice, Captain."

"Do you know your destination?" Devi wasn't a fool. She could see who held the long stick, and it wasn't her.

"Verboten—"

"No!" Devi sucked in her breath, afraid to reveal the depth of her revulsion at that name. It was a death world.

"So, we do it the hard way?" Agrippa's eyes narrowed, and he held the cigar immobilized in the air waiting on her answer.

"Verboten." She knew the tales, the excessive magnetic fields, the gravity well that would buffet their ship's ARD, the poisonous air, the *absolute danger* of that place, and she knew she didn't have a choice. Her ship was capable. It was her crew that she worried about.

"So, yes or no? I want to go get my men."

"If you will let my crew run my ship, I will do this. And my crew remains aboard when we reach Verboten. Each one, that is, unless Engineer Apinelu wishes to join you on world." She hissed the words, and she saw the engineer flinch.

Good, Devi said to herself. *And die there for your betrayal.*

It was a mean thought, and she didn't know if Mata Vaishnodevi would overlook her insolence, but she was certain Maa Durga would happily shred the engineer's heart and drink her blood to balance the evil Apinelu had done to the *Putin.*

—Chapter 27—

Interdicted Colony World *Verboten*

Recon, Army Support Personnel
. . . in which a new plan rises to the surface

"PYRO. OR DO YOU prefer Loki?"

I looked at Pyro, grinning, and hoping for a response. I intended my words to cut into his good nature and bring a bantering response.

"I don't mind." He turned to me from inside his green helmet, and his suit's shoulders shrugged.

"Man up." I gripped my hand into a fist and brought it sideways against his shoulder. Any other man would have fallen down, possibly with a broken arm or dislocated joint. My exoskeleton would have seen to that. Not Pyro. We were evenly matched, and my hit would do him no harm. The fact was, he barely shifted his position, and I knew I had my actuators set for a punishing level of force. They were calibrated to the weight of the Cask, and I hadn't turned them down since we'd paused to take a rest.

"Leave it. We have other business."

I looked to my side to see Ghost's red face through his visor. His tone was unmistakable.

"That means?" It was early, but I knew what was coming. Perhaps it was time. Ghost would know.

"Weapons ready. Pyro, got that?"

My heart thumped with anticipation, and I glanced at the sky. I would know it when I saw it. These fools around me. They hadn't understood anything, but they would now. I clicked through my weapons, making sure each was live. The plan had been to play it to the end, allowing the Envoy to feel safe before the inevitable conclusion. Now, a new plan was to be put into play. I looked for the silvery man-thing and failed to locate it. I expected it to be the hardest to kill.

"Yeah," Pyro muttered. "Just waiting on fresh battle options from Recon, if he has any."

"Oh, I've got them," I retorted. I triggered his feed. The plan poured into his database, and I watched his expression grow hard with antici-pation. The signal for us to strike would be the appearance of the Ship.

Far overhead, the pinpoint flash of meteors peppered the sky. The Ship. The rush of adrenalin was almost unbearable, even if my plan suggested we might not all make it through alive.

—Chapter 28—

Dreadnaught *Vladimir Vladimirovich Putin*

First Mate August Murphy
. . . in which a bitter brew makes for a sour cup of tea

FIRST MATE MURPHY stepped through the lift doors. For the briefest moment, the scene was a familiar one, with Captain Devi in her chair, seeming to be doing very ordinary Captain things.

Then, in a glance, he caught the opposing lift, the damaged doors that had been forced from their tracks by the endorphin-infused clones he'd attempted to beat back earlier. His arm wrapped in its sling was a bitter reminder of how that had gone. That lift was useless until the *Putin* had access to a naval shipyard for refitment.

He stepped up just behind Devi, at an angle so he could be seen but not obscure her view of the Bridge. He put one arm behind his back and found the motion awkward with the other one in a sling.

His hand floundered for a moment before he dropped it at his side.

"Murphy on the Bridge, ma'am." Like old times. Like yesterday. Like when this ship was theirs and not controlled by mutineers.

"Ah, Murphy. Things seem to be going well, if not exactly under our control."

"Yes, ma'am. If I had the doing of this again, ma'am—"

"I know. We all feel that way. We'd do it differently, each of us."

Her prayer cloth slipped into her sleeve, and she rose from her seat with an effortless control that suggested the fury of a caged Bengal tiger. They weren't native in his beloved Ireland, but the Captain had shared stories about her experiences with them.

"You have the Bridge, Murphy."

"I have the Bridge, Captain."

He didn't look as she exited. He was the acting captain, now, and that was what mattered. Anyway, the two soldiers with their massive exoskeletons at either side of the lift doors were a reminder he didn't need. Their blank eyes, their unnaturally smooth faces. Almost effeminate, never the need to shave, boys with the bodies of men, grown to vat specs and given the power to wreak havoc on everything they touched.

Yeah, he'd do it differently if he had the doing

of it again. The *Putin* commandeered. Reports of the Army's Training Officer hijacked. Word was that the man wasn't human, although Murphy didn't see how that was possible. He looked human enough, if cruel and sadistic, but that was the Army's problem. Well, it *had* been the Army's problem. Who controlled him? His guess was Ali, the Army's Commo. That shunt rig of his, but how? The Army team seemed to be able to communicate with a private Net the ship couldn't access. He had Ivanova and Hansen working on it, but all they could say was that they could sense something going on over their heads, some sort of Uppernet. What, maybe they could tell him with more time. If Jónsdóttir were there to help them . . . but that wasn't to be for some time with the wounds the man had received.

The real problem was that they didn't have more time. Murphy had a clearer idea of Agrippa's intent, now. The General's men, sure, he wanted to recover them, but only after they had completed their "mission" with the Envoy, whatever that happened to be.

Murphy's guess, not something he'd be glad to uncover, once he did.

Second Helmsman Papadopoulos, having replaced Quispe at his console, turned to catch Murphy's eye.

"Helmsman?" Murphy lifted one eyebrow.

"Do we—" Papadopoulos licked his bottom lip. His hands hovered over his controls. His thick neck and heavy features suggested something ominous about to happen.

"Careful, Helmsman." Murphy had seen the destruction foisted on the Commanding Officer, and he knew of what Müller was capable. He didn't intend to spark something he couldn't extinguish, especially with two clone exos standing on the Bridge.

"Change course. They'll never know until it's too late."

Murphy noticed his hands. The symbols under his fingers could be the start of a course correction that would be satisfying but ultimately disastrous. Until Ivanova and Hansen had something, they didn't know what the Army knew, but Murphy knew they had shut the ship down without so much as a whimper or a by your leave.

"Not now, Helmsman. It's not the time."

"But, sir." Papadopoulos' eyes were red with desperation and anger. "I can do this. Let me."

"Helmsman Papadopoulos," and Murphy stood, his massive shoulders pulsing with authority and presence, "consider yourself relieved. Navigator John, please take the helmsman's position."

He turned away from Papadopoulos, refusing to let the man see that he wanted to give him permission. If he left him on duty, and

Papadopoulos asked again, he might relent.

"Sir."

Murphy turned to see Papadopoulos at his side.

"August, sir, we can't let them win. We must do *something*. A course change will give us at least some time to come up with a plan."

"And we will have a plan, Ceasar. Now is not the time. Please exit the Bridge."

"This is not over, sir." The man's face was black with fury. "You know that."

"Now, Helmsman." He nodded to the lift, and at the same time, he was aware that John was fully focused on her console and the screen just before her. He was certain she was taking in every word.

As the Helmsman approached the lift, the doors whooshed open, and General Agrippa stepped through. Papadopoulos moved aside, his eyes down, waiting as CSO Finola de Jong and CSO Zilpah al-Din trailed Agrippa in. Once they were inside, Papadopoulos brushed through the door, glaring at Murphy, as the doors sealed him away.

"Smart move, Murphy." Agrippa seemed to be carrying the cigar everywhere, as though now that he had nominal command of the ship, the space inside was his to use as he pleased.

"Sir?" Murphy still stood, and he cut his glance Agrippa's direction. He offered no salute or other indication of the man's authority on the Bridge.

"Come now, Officer. You sent him away

because he wanted to divert the ship on an alternate course. You think I'm unaware of that? Give me credit."

"Sir." Murphy didn't know how the man knew that. If Ivanova and Hansen could just get a break . . . but then, maybe it was too late for that.

"I see Devi didn't see fit to stay for the show."

"The show, sir?" Murphy didn't like the sound of that.

"You think she turned over command because you could do a better job? That woman is your better a hundred times over, even if it galls me to admit it. She knew you wouldn't hinder my people, meaning she's smarter than she gives herself credit. Move aside, Officer Murphy. It's time for my people to do their job."

de Jong smoothly installed herself at the Weapons console, and al-Din moved up behind John and cleared her throat. John looked at Murphy and waited for him to nod before standing and allowing the Combat Systems Officer to slide into her seat.

Murphy considered. There were none of his people at the ship's controls, not anywhere throughout the *Putin*. The vessel could run itself on automatics, even think for itself in limited engagements, so that wasn't a worry—and was the reason so few people were on the Bridge. Agrippa had most of the crew confined to quarters. None of the *Putin*'s crew had been given inside information, except perhaps Engineer Apinelu, who had chosen her side early on, and she wasn't a trusted source, anyway.

al-Din keyed the console. "Hey, Commo, you got my position?"

The console buzzed a moment, then Murphy heard, "Ali, here. That you, al-Din?"

"Jar head. Who do you think? This is the hardline we're using. de Jong's on Weapons. Set up her permissions. Full access. I'm running the drops. Ready for de Jong's signal?"

"Yah, always. Tell her to key the console."

al-Din nodded, and de Jong reached to her console.

"You been having fun with al-Din in the wires, plugged-in lover boy?" She chuckled and winked at al-Din.

"Been on her Construct like white on rice, and the little gem doesn't even know. I've got your location. Be aware I've got Müller idling for now, so he's offline. Don't depend on him until we get our men on the ground. Copy."

"Müller's offline. Copy. And First Mate Murphy knows and so does, um, Navigator John?" She glanced at the Navigator. There was no reason to treat the *Putin*'s crew with less than complete respect, and when John nodded, de Jong gave her console her full attention.

"Oops. Sorry." Ali didn't sound sorry.

"Not a problem, lover boy. They ain't goin' nowhere til this songbird's done sung its song. Let's get our soldiers on the ground. Back to al-Din."

"al-Din, Commo. We're coming in hot to the planet. We're looking at—" She paused and looked off to the side as if in contact with someone elsewhere in the ship. After a moment, she seemed to reengage. "—gravity at least one point four and an ungodly magnetic field. You might want to route extra power to the ARDs. This is going to be a rough ride."

"Got that. Are the footies masked up?" There were one hundred of each class of clone: Sam, Jake, and Mike class, each further identified by number. "The info I've got says this world's atmosphere'll do no one any good. Don't want our boys to hit the ground, then hit the ground, if you know what I mean." He chuckled over the feed.

"Enough of this." General Agrippa's growl silenced the conversation. "Can you hear me over the comm, Commo?"

"Just like in your head. What are you thinking, General?"

"That city down there. What is it?"

"St. Petersburg, sir." It seemed the Commo was well versed on Verboten, even if his manner was careless and off the cuff.

"That one. That's where Hernandez would head. Drop our troops there. Those buildings are perfect cover. Can we do that on one pass and bring in the ship's firepower to mop up stragglers on the next?"

"My plan exactly, General. Great minds think alike."

"And you, Commo, are full of it. Agrippa out."

The General turned to glare at Murphy. Murphy steeled himself for what was about to come.

"These two." He pointed with two fingers on one hand at the same time, taking in al-Din and de Jong. "In control. Got that?"

Murphy ground his teeth and refused to reply.

"I'll take that for a yes. It better be if your Captain wants this ship back when this is over. al-Din, I'm headed down to check on my men. Make sure they're racked up and ready to fly." At the lift doors, he spoke to the two guards. "Those two even look like they're interfering, I want them incapacitated."

"Sir," came the stereophonic reply.

Once he was gone, the speakers at the Helmsman's station started up with a nervous laugh.

"al-Din, we can do that, right? What the General said? I expect you can guess better than me."

"We've got this, Commo. Better me than you.

At least I know what I'm doing."

Murphy looked at the two women at the consoles, and he took in the two guards with their beefy exoskeletons. He wished *he* knew what they were doing. What he imagined was as wild as a North Sea winter, and he was beginning to wonder if the Envoy was intended to survive.

His stomach churned, and the taste crawled up his throat.

—Chapter 29—

Interdicted Colony World *Verboten*

Freshly Toasted Footies
*. . . who discover exposed exoskeletons are fine
for space*

RACKED UP IN SETS OF twenty, ten on each side, Mikes with Mikes, Jakes with Jakes, and Sams with Sams, the expendable foot soldiers—clones—outfitted in their fully charged exoskeletons and wearing face shields and atmospheric breathers, dropped into the line one rack at a time with a grinding clank of chains and gears. As their feet dangled just below the open fuselage, the wind whipped their rip proof clothing as if to tear it from their skin.

The rack released each group, twenty at a time, and they plummeted feet first through Verboten's thin thermosphere, headed at ever-increasing speeds towards the planet's thickening stratosphere.

CASK

They hoped—if vat-grown military clones could be said to hope—they all made it down in one piece.

When all thirteen sets were away—the Mikes, Jakes, and Sams—the launching drone's thick deployment bay door lurched, and clanking and jerking with chain-driven gears, the doors wound themselves upward until they crashed into the body of the drone. There was no one on board, so who cared about the niceties of airtight seals and the gentle kiss of metal door to metal hull? Drones were expendable, and who cared if they appreciated the nicer things in life or not?

The drone's reusable rockets kicked in, and at more gees than living cells could endure, it bled its lifeblood as it sped after the *Putin,* determined to reach and lodge in her hold for the next deployment it would be required to perform.

The air as the soldiers shot groundward burned their exposed skin, a high price to pay to stand on Verboten's deadly surface. Then, toast—lightly browned, please—is good when served up just right, and these soldiers wore armor that would serve them well when they sat down to breakfast with the crew and passengers of the ship they had chased half across the galaxy.

They entered the troposphere, thick and soupy, and it pulled at their tightly fitting face masks, occasionally leaking, but there was nothing anyone could do. They were preoccupied with the wind screaming through their flapping shoe straps, tugging at various weapons tightly lashed to legs, torsos, and of course to their exoskeletons.

Then, there was the upcoming landing to steal away their attention. Their exoskeletons were designed to make the landing as survivable as possible, but Verboten was big, and her gravity was 1.4 Earth normal. Skin burned, air screamed, and it was impossible to see how close they were to the ground. Readouts in their masks gave them some clue, if they could focus enough to make out the rapidly changing numbers as their face shields vibrated and shook with the vortex of air beating at their bodies.

Moisture peeled from the soldiers' clothing and off their face masks, as each clone became a small cloudlet; then the water whipped away in roaring vortexes as the air thickened up and began to heat their lower extremities. Just before the ground leaped up to slam into their extended legs, hollow breakaway rods shot out of the bottoms of their exoskeletons, designed to act as air brakes, then to collapse as the soldiers slammed into the ground, absorbing the massive velocities they had attained.

The soldiers fought their exoskeletons as they shuddered with the fury of braking from full speed to something approaching a survivable landing.

One other defense against gravity was set to

CASK

deploy just before each soldier slammed leg-first onto the ground. The superheated air sluicing along their bodies would ignite a short-lived retrorocket buried in the breakaway rods acting as air brakes. As planned, meters from the ground, five-hundred-twenty miniature suns ignited, flared for a few seconds, and flashed out of existence.

Then, the ground jumped up and met them.

The hollow rods collapsed as intended for those troops landing on hard surfaces, such as streets, parking lots, or bridges, and broke away immediately as each soldier's exoskeleton contorted in a preprogramed manner to allow the wearer to roll and dissipate as much energy as possible. For those lucky enough to land on soil, the rods buried themselves in the ground, absorbing just enough momentum to prevent incapacitating bone breakage.

Internal organ damage was impossible to mitigate, except with powered body sleeves that cinched the soldier's torso like an airbag for that fraction of a second of impact. It worked, mostly.

Those with broken legs or ruptured spleens tore across the ground with the rest, pumped full of stimulants that overrode any sensation of pain. That was what their exoskeletons were for; bones not necessary.

A few lay where they fell, casualties of a high-altitude deployment. The risk went with the duty of being a soldier, even if they were clones and had little choice in the matter.

Two-hundred-fifty-seven footies on the ground. Not bad. In any military deployment, a one-percent loss ratio was perfectly acceptable, as those still afoot and breathing assured themselves.

Most landed in or near the city, hitting in parks, on roads, and a number making their entrance directly through the roofs of buildings. Each carried a digital download of their targets. Open season, wasn't that how it was said? Across internal viewscreens, the information repeatedly scrolled down the inside of the footies' face shields, with names, biometric descriptions, and images for verification of each kill.

Captain Vicente Falco, a handsome fellow by anyone's measure, his face filled with fire and zeal.

First Mate Jiang Song, a dark-haired beauty with a teasing light in her eye.

Medical Officer Richard Franklin, wearing a Med-Tab at his throat.

Science Officer Aldrik Jollenbeck, his wasted body trapped in a high-tech wheelchair.

Engineer Sanaa Nakato Ssanyu, her split personality concocted from an African genetic database.

Bishop Silvestre Zubizarreta, heavy, with swaths of florid skin padding his face.

A boy listed only as the Acolyte, even in the

image hidden in a hooded robe.

The Cygnian Diplomatic Envoy was their prize. His was the image of his medical life-support Cask. He wasn't theirs to rescue, but to ensure he never made it to Earth.

Their lists overlooked four passengers on the *Franklin Delano Roosevelt.*

The Android, who was of course the ship when connected and able to mutate into various forms at any time when fully powered. In truth, it was unlikely anyone alive anywhere near Verboten would live to see its power source fully exhausted.

The last three were Ghost, Recon, and Pyro, known aboard the *Putin as* Hernandez, McAvoy, and Nissen. They were on the "to be rescued" list. They were the General's special team, and he wanted to bring them home.

Finally aground, the foot soldiers did what all good foot soldiers did when tasked with securing an area. They searched for the highest vantage points. Doors that wouldn't open, they were easy. If they needed to go through walls, well, that's what their exoskeletons were for. Up they climbed, higher and higher, until they located the best windows for vantage points, searching for those destined to become casualties of war.

One of the Mikes, sporting the sharp Nordic features and blond hair of all the Mikes, and boasting the number twenty-seven on his breather mask, exoskeleton, and torso, dropped against a wall inside the upper level of one of the city's buildings. Which building was unimportant, if it was high and offered a superior vantage point to take out their targets.

"They warmed us for this?" Mike27's exoskeleton whirred and thumped with mechanical solidity each time he moved, except for one wrist. He could silence the noises, set the rig to stealth mode, but it slowed him down and drained power quicker. He wanted it to whir and thump. He liked the feel.

"For what?" Jake62—easily identified as a Jake-class clone by his peaches-and-cream skin and jet hair—turned to look out the window, giving off whirring noises and thumping sounds of his own.

"This rig." Mike27 reached to one wrist, made an adjustment, and cursed as the joint threw a spark. He rotated his hand, testing the mechanical joint, and when it seemed to work, he turned his attention to the view beyond the glass.

"The magnetic field." Jake62 held viewers to his eyes, shaking it when the device hit his face shield, muttering, "I could *see* if I didn't have to have this *breather* on my face."

"Not if you're dead."

Mike and Jake turned to see another Mike and two Jakes joining them. The speaker was a Sam,

CASK

identified by his rash of prominent freckles and coarse ginger hair.

"Who made you God?" Mike27 snorted with a laugh. "Any problems with your rig?"

"Yeah, it's in the same room with you." Sam03 walked to the window, his exoskeleton kicking up dust as it planted his feet hard on the floor. He could see across the alley to other windows. A laser flashed from one, then again, and Sam03 retrieved a black laser pen from a sealed pocket and flashed back in the same pattern.

"Hold this position," Sam03 said. "On the horizon, that must be the *Roosevelt*." Black smoke dirtied the distant ridge. "There's nowhere for them to come but right through here. This should be easy."

"What you Sams always say." Jake62 laughed, his clear skin giving him a boyish look behind his face shield. His arms said differently, like he could manage without his exosuit, and he'd have no trouble at all.

"It's why we always take point. If we let you chumps run the show, it *would* be hard. Weapons out and ready, men. Memorize your list of targets. No loose ends, and that's from the General."

"Sir!" Mike27 gave a mock salute, jerking his rig erect, while remaining on his knees. "Sir, yessir!"

"You Mikes are all the same. Guess that's

clone territory, and I should expect it. At ease."

"Thank you, sir," and the Mike clone fell back against the wall, laughing. His wrist hung up again, and he shook it to get it working before grasping a collapsible rifle from his armature and pulling it loose.

"Eyes up," Sam03 said, touching his face with two fingers and pointing to the view out the window. The spire of a cathedral punched the sky, and just beyond, a dry fountain centered a barren courtyard. "No clone left behind."

He turned and exited through the door, followed by the Mike and two Jakes with him. Mike27 did note that the knee on one of the Jakes caught and jumped with each step.

"Worked fine in space," Mike mumbled.

"What's that?" Jake was attaching the stock onto his collapsible rifle. He didn't look up.

"Nothing," Mike said. "Just thinking how much fun it's going to be when we get back in space."

"In stasis, you mean. What's the fun in that?" Jake looked up this time, and he had an impish twinkle in his eye. "That Song's a looker. I wonder how quickly she has to die."

Mike looked to his weapon. He'd thought the same thing. It wasn't going to happen, though. If he knew his clones—and he *was* one!—there were a couple hundred soldiers on this planet thinking the same thing.

After all, what Mike27 thought, every Mike thought. And that went for all the Jakes and Sams, too.

There were a few drawbacks to being a clone footie, and this was one. Mostly, though, it was all right. A hundred brothers, all just like him. And when it came time to party, they knew how to make it happen.

"Yeah, Jake, who you thinking to take out first?" Mike looked up to see Jake testing the fit of his rifle against his shoulder and peering down the sight.

"I want the kid. Pow, pow." Jake jerked the muzzle up with each pow.

"Perverted, or needing an easy kill?"

"The second. And the first. Anyway, can't be on my conscience killing a kid if I can't see his face."

"I want the Envoy. That'd make the General happy."

"Him and me, too. Then we can get back to our war."

"Well said." Mike clicked open his magazine and began to insert his ammunition. "You and me, Jake62."

—Chapter 30—

Interdicted Colony World *Verboten*

Android

. . . in which intent is a finger in a dike

[[INDIGENOUS PLANT. Interesting! **Flow-er** Olfactory sample required.]]

The Android knelt, drew in a deep breath, and sighed, just the way a man might when coming upon something that triggers an especially good memory, one initiated by an olfactory interaction, that is, by a smell. His sigh, however, was to pass the volatile chemicals from the flower across his internal sensory array, so that he could differentiate each variation of odors into specific categories to help him make sense of why the flower grew in that particular location. In this case, he caught a whiff of chlorofluorocarbon, revealing a stunted level of technological advancement. Safer propellants were easily discoverable, and only primitive cultures used the dangerous ones.

CASK

He walked, sampling the various aspects of his new environment, each element encountered recorded as batches of data for later retrieval. He'd noted the broken wall at the entrance to the city, brushing a silver-black finger across the rough surface, his sampling spikes absorbing a minute amount of crushed concrete. From it, he learned the planet's industrial base still used crushed and burned limestone as part of a sand mixture, without the usual chemicals normally found in advanced cement blends. He was unable to tell if it was because of a deteriorated knowledge base (entirely possible with the colony's history) or lack of available resources. The levels of volatiles were quite high.

[[Accessing information! Viewing Daimler-Porsche exclusivity agreements to mine calcium silicates, aluminates, and ferrites from the surface of Verboten. Accessing complete!]]

That told him the issue wasn't available resources; it was likely recovery methods. A society had to be able to harvest its resources to be able to use them. Across a wide avenue, the Medical Officer stood unmoving, gazing up at a larger than life three-dimensional carving on the face of a towering building. Higher, in the curve of the sky, a brace of shooting stars littered the heavens. The Android mentally severed his connection with his sampling spikes, withdrawing the hair-like manifestations into his silver-black skin, and leaving his unblemished fingertips slightly ridged for grasp and adhesion. In the same thought, he triggered a cascading process of relays, causing the signal to trip other electronic relays, the electronic spark tumbling in a predictable pattern from the gross to the minute, until locating Franklin's glass and getting permission to have a conversation.

[[Franklin, truly a primitive society. Inquiry. Detecting atmospheric residue, possibly dangerous to organic life. Wish to know more about Verboten's accessible technological resources when arriving on planet. Am certain knowledge was high and technology was low. Also, am registering unexpected meteor shower. Might explain atmospheric residue. End inquiry.]]

The missive was short, but it implied more, much of which the Android hadn't needed to share with Franklin's glass. Being the ship's Android implied a higher set of thinking skills, a level of processing that few other constructed organisms could match. An inquiry from the Android was never simply for information. He might look calm and serene with his chiseled silver-black face, or totally connected with his many arms, or extremely proficient when transformed into a mobile hospital surgery ward, but his brain was always thinking, evaluating, and concluding. If the Android asked a question, it was a steppingstone in the elaborately terraced construction that masqueraded as thoughts in that silver-black head.

Not surprisingly, Franklin glanced down at his glass, then up, his eyes searching for a moment. Puzzled, he found the Android, and his expression softened into a brief smile. He nodded his head, then turned back to the figure on the building and walked forward to ascend the steps. The Medical Officer made no attempt to reply, but as the message hadn't been a direct request, but rather an observation with a general interest inquiry attached, the man's behavior wasn't off-putting or surprising. As Franklin disappeared into the shadowed doorway, the Android turned at a noise. He turned down his visual acuity sensors and focused on his auditory receptors. The noise was faint, a mere vibration of the ground under his feet, with an echoing resonance penetrating the air around him. He let his artificial brain matter access his stored reference files, for a moment regretting his lack of access to the ship's more extensive resources, but almost immediately letting the irrational response slip from him. Regret was a human attribute, one to be feigned when in contact with his meat and jelly compadres, but totally useless in the real world. Regret didn't undo the realities of the situation, and therefore, it was a useless trait that had no place in a structured being's thinking process.

Extending sampling spikes from the soles of his feet, he noted the wave pattern of the vibrations in the paving, the living heartbeat of an ominous and unseen beast. The meteor shower from earlier? He judged the decrease from one foot to the other, accessed an algorithm to determine the direction and distance of the source, and turned down an empty, shadowed alleyway. The cornices of the opposing buildings hunkered over him, as if crouching expectantly, blocking all sun after the first meter or so. The Android hardly noticed as his eyes flickered, adjusting to the ambient light, and brightening the entire scene. The windows lining the multi-story passageway reflected what they saw, as if looking into one another's deepest thoughts, and seeing what was hidden there.

The Android walked along, focused on the source of the sound and oblivious to the windows, even as they seemed to follow his every move.

CASK

—Chapter 31—

Dreadnaught *Vladimir Vladimirovich Putin*

Weapons Officer Finola de Jong
. . . who prepares to crush a very small worm

"AL-DIN TO ROSSI. Drop away. Confirm, Rossi."

Ops de Jong watched al-Din expectantly, her hand over the comm, waiting for confirmation from Auxiliaries Officer Blythe Rossi.

Rossi was the Army officer assigned to monitor Technician Kai Kumar, who had been ordered by Captain Devi to step in for Operations Officer Ulric Jónsdóttir after his disastrous and misguided attempt to defend Engineer Saskia Kazlauskas during the Army's takeover of the *Putin*.

Kazlauskas was fine and had been conscripted to help with the drop. Jónsdóttir would need weeks in recovery before he was of use to the ship once more.

Kumar knew the *Putin* better than anyone on

the Army team. He managed the avionics and sensors, exactly what the General needed to get his troops accurately placed on the ground with as few casualties as possible. de Jong had expected resistance from the technician, but Kumar had capitulated readily at Devi's orders. Still, de Jong didn't trust any of the *Putin*'s crew, and each crewmember on duty for this exercise was closely monitored by one of Agrippa's team.

"That's a go for deployment. Thirteen racks away."

"The situation there. All okay?" al-Din glanced sideways to de Jong. de Jong chuckled. It had better be, with four troops in full exo gear monitoring the drop to ensure the deployment went smoothly.

"Right as rain. One thing, a query from Engineer Kazlauskas. I tried to ping the Medical Bay to check on Jónsdóttir for her and nothing. Why the switch to hardline?"

"We're being jammed. Popa thought this might happen and suggested we use Ali's shunt to run all communications on the ship's hardline. We already controlled it before the takeover, so, as awkward as it is, it's secure."

"As we can make it." Rossi laughed sourly. "When will we know about the *Roosevelt* team? Any contact with them yet?"

"Negative. We have visual confirmation on the

Roosevelt. Whatever Hernandez did, the ship is shredded. For now, we wait on the footies to find them so we can bring them home."

"Thanks. If that's all, Rossi out."

"al-Din out."

During the conversation, Pilot-in-Command Kaua'i Mori had joined them to step in when the *Putin* began maneuvers within Verboten's atmosphere. He slipped past the chair and took an empty console. With First Helmsman Quispe off duty and Second Helmsman Papadopoulos relieved from the Bridge for near insubordination, he had no one to oversee.

"Zilpah, how long before you expect an update on our men from the *Roosevelt?*" de Jong glanced at the two crew from the *Putin* now seated on the floor and back to al-Din. "If someone else asks . . . you know. I'd like to be able to offer something positive."

The lights across the Bridge went dark before al-Din could reply. A siren blared, and after about a minute, red emergency lighting flickered on along the lower sections of the wall. Murphy and John were still in place, as was everyone else. As soon as the emergency lights came on, and they could make out the controls on the consoles, the two women began attempting contact with the rest of the ship. Mori tried also, punching in every override he knew before dropping to the floor and pulling a panel under the console free. He tugged at a module and wrestled until it came free, setting a small fire going. He ripped off his shirt and smothered it. He sat back at the console, tapped a combination of icons, and the lights flickered back on across the Bridge. Almost immediately, the lift doors opened, and General Agrippa came in hard.

"What happened to my ship? Someone in here had better know."

Mori stood and turned, one side of his face blackened, and his shirt crumpled and on the floor at his feet. "Sir, I don't know who, but I know what. I overrode it the only way possible. The system is rebooting now. I'm sorry sir, but we may not get back everything without rebuilding part of the system. I suspect I shorted out a few boards."

"Your shirt, Mori? You can explain that, too?" The General cleared his throat with a loud grunt.

"Yessir. A bit of a fire. It's out."

"Son, the Army could use a few more like you. Get your shirt back on and let's see what's still working. And get those fools off this Bridge." He pointed to Murphy and John without looking.

"Comm's back online, sir." de Jong tapped her console, and several lights blinked on. Then she turned in her chair and smiled. "But I don't think we're going to need it any longer. Whatever Mori did, he also killed the jamming mechanism. I'm calling an escort for Officer Murphy and Navigator

John."

She did notice a lag in the Uppernet, so it wasn't perfect, but she could get through. That was better than the oh-so-slow-manual system that ran along the ship's fiberlines.

It didn't take long to uncover the culprit behind the power failure on the Bridge. The angry Papadopoulos hadn't been satisfied with Murphy, and he'd meant it when he said this wasn't over. He'd convinced Technician Ivanova to help him start a program running that would shut down access from the Bridge to the rest of the ship. Mori's quick actions had isolated the program, killed that section of the ship's computational systems, mitigated the damage, and kept the Bridge mostly functional.

The lift doors opened, and Traino Kasem Müller stepped in. Whether under Ali's direct control or operating under limited autonomy, it wasn't clear. What was clearer was the weapon in his hand. He motioned, Murphy and John joined him, and the three disappeared into the lift.

"Down there." Agrippa had his hands behind his back, and a cigar back in his mouth, whether the same or different, it was hard to tell. No one had seen it appear. "Are my troops on the ground? I want to know what's happening."

Agrippa spoke aloud, as de Jong expected, staying off the Uppernet. She could see the strain on his face as a rush of queries about the status of their situation began to ping in his head. As it was only Army personnel present at the time, using the Net was not only unnecessary but unwise. Few people were good enough to maintain conversations and monitor multiple information feeds at the same time. Keep it simple, people, the General often said. That way no one goes off half-cocked and fewer people die.

It was his people he meant, but that was understood.

In addition to efforts to contact the surface, additional queries began flooding the Uppernet, wondering what was going on with the ship's systems. Basic functions were failing across the board, and not all were rebooting.

"General, sir, I have contact with the surface." Pilot Mori held his hand over his console, as though ready to complete a connection. Surprisingly, he wore a speaker in his ear. He winced once as though what he heard was either frightfully loud or devastatingly unbelievable.

"I'm not getting any closer to my war just standing here. Let's hear it, Pilot." The General's face tightened as the end of his cigar glowed, and he cut his eyes to al-Din and back to Mori.

Mori touched his console, and an unfamiliar voice broke into the room.

". . . whatever it is, there's no stopping it. I've

already lost twelve men in this quadrant alone. Is anyone up there? General, Commo, anyone—"

"Soldier, this is General Agrippa. Get hold of yourself. Who am I speaking with, and what's there that you can't stop?"

"Sorry, General. Er, yessir. This is Corporal Mike47. We were making good progress with our targets. Good kills, too. Clean, like we should. Then this thing came out of nowhere. Whatever we throw at it, it changes. I swear, sir, it morphs into whatever it wants to be. We can't battle this, sir, not with the weapons at our disposal."

"Can you list your kills for me, Corporal?" The General nodded at al-Din, and she brought up the list from the troops' faceplates.

"Some, sir, maybe all. Let me check." His voice seemed farther away as he called, "Mike, um, 19, who's down? Can you get that for me?" In the background, weapons rattled, pinged, and hissed. Something big was going on.

"Yessir. Let me see . . ." —fainter, someone else's voice— ". . . everyone except Falco is either eliminated or incapacitated. Oh, that boy, the Acolyte. We've got him pinned in the cathedral, but there's no exit, so count him eliminated as soon as we flush him out."

"You get that General?" Mike47's voice boomed into the room as if talking over background noise.

"Loud and clear. You're a good soldier, son. Keep up the good work. Agrippa out."

"Thank you, sir. Mike out."

The General let out a hard breath, taking his time, and locking his eyes on Mori.

"General?" de Jong spoke softly. He looked like he knew exactly was happening, and he was coming to a decision.

"Okay, Mori. You're about to earn your pay. You know what an Android is?"

"Yessir. Müller's one. A robot."

"And that's why I'm commanding this mission and you're not, Lieutenant. You and that wooden leg of yours—" Clearly, he knew it was titanium. "—are about to get schooled. That ship down there," and he pointed towards the floor of the Bridge, "was one of the most advanced Interstellar Rangers built. The Android—not a robot, son—is the control nexus of the ship, totally connected at all times and able to mutate into various forms, most of them deadly to human life. I had hoped it died with the ship. That's what we're fighting down there, and we need the full firepower from this vessel if we want to eliminate it. You get to take us down."

"Yessir." Mori, his shirt rumpled and covered with soot, and his face blackened on one side, drew up to his console. He began to log in protocols that would give him command of the ship's naviga-

CASK

tional computers.

"al-Din, you know everything there is to know about the *Vladimir Putin*. At least I hope you do. I need the full complement of firepower available on this vessel. I'll blast the surface of that planet into glass if that's what it takes, but I want that thing dead."

"Yessir." She turned to de Jong. "Finola, are you ready to plug in?"

"Now's as good a time as ever." de Jong slipped a small case from her breast pocket and laid it on her console. From inside, she unrolled about a meter of hyper-thin wire. She lifted out an adaptor, slotted it into the console, and powered it on. The adaptor glowed red for a bit then turned green. de Jong touched the side, and the device whispered, "Accessing systems. You are now connected. You may insert your hyper-wire at your convenience."

de Jong threaded one end of the wire into the adaptor device, and she pulled her left eye wide with one hand and threaded the other end of the hyper-wire into the center of her eyeball, working it in until the adaptor dinged.

"You are now in control of Weapons Tracking and Control."

"Ready," de Jong said, both her hands on her console, and her eyes on control panels and gauges no one else in the room could see. "Mori, take us in. I'll do the rest."

"Thrusting now."

Mori, as Pilot-in-Command, was fully in control of the *Putin* until the exercise was over. de Jong accepted that. However, she was in control of Weapons, and that was better by far.

CASK

—Chapter 32—

Interdicted Colony World *Verboten*

Captain Vicente Falco

. . . who finds a beam is as good as a berm

"SONG, IS THE ENVOY SAFE?" I threw myself through a broken doorway as yet another red laser sliced away half of a building, revealing fully furnished rooms severed like an artery and spewing bricks, furniture, and lighting fixtures into the street.

I had pulled my short-range portable comm from my pocket and clipped it to my collar. I had no doubt Firstie had done the same. It was why she was my First Mate. She could think smart even as she could prod me into being better than I thought I was. I needed a little prodding right now. What had I missed? Nothing, I thought, yet my ship hunkered on the horizon, broken and shredded, and now, I was losing crew and passengers as quickly as that massive ship overhead could slice them down.

Still, the Envoy. It must be protected at all costs. I hoped Song had the answer I hoped for. I thought of Elvis, that long-ago king of rock who had died on his toilet at 42. I often thought of him as my hero, if a rock god who died on the toilet can be a hero, but he had lived a life of godlike proportions. I was beginning to think I'd not make 42, not with the way my day was going.

I shivered, and I wiped sweat from my face. The trauma falling from the skies, and now this. I recalled why Verboten was proscribed. It wasn't just her wildly erratic magnetic field. Fine time to remember, although there was nothing I could have done about it if I had.

A cough shook my chest, and when I spit, I left traces of blood.

"Song?" I touched my comm at my throat. Touching upped the signal while I touched it. Doing so drained power faster, but it didn't seem that was going to matter much longer.

"Song here."

The words came through in a ragged gasp, and I picked up the pop of small arms fire. We were on a diplomatic mission. We didn't carry weapons, except for the Android, and he wasn't really a weapon, not in the military sense. If I could hear weapons fire over Song's comm, it was close. The comm, although portable and very small, filtered out almost everything except for vocals.

"The Envoy?" I repeated my request. She would understand my focus on our Cygnian traveler. I wanted to ask about her, how she was making out, but she didn't require sympathy and wouldn't accept it if I offered.

"Sorry, sir. Hold."

The long hiss of an energy weapon burned through the comm. I thought she was gone, and I felt my heart drain the blood from my hands. I flexed them to make sure they were still attached to my arms.

"One more who won't get in my way." The words barked from my comm with satisfaction.

"Song?" Relief flooded me. "You have a weapon?"

"Yessir. Android's been a miracle, taking down our attackers right and left. One didn't need his weapon and I did. So, there you go." She laughed, but I heard the sour note. There was nothing amusing about taking a dead man's weapon to make more dead men.

"The Envoy . . ." I hated to insist, but there it was.

"Right. In the Android's care, and that's the best we can hope for." She coughed. "My chest. If these suckers from the sky don't get me, this cough might. Sir, I watched Jolley go. You would be proud. He made the most of his magnetic lift, ramming two attackers, and I think incapacitating their exoskeletons. Anyway, they didn't get back up. He gave Sister and Franklin an opportunity for escape."

"Good, they are safe." For a time, I thought the soldiers accompanying us would assist us when we realized the meteor shower and the impacts we heard were of manmade origin. Vat grown, I now knew, but then, we were oblivious. Who could have expected it, Verboten, proscribed and lost for a century? No ship was allowed near, not even the *Roosevelt*, except that we had no other choice.

The Android was our first warning. He felt the impacts initially, and even he didn't understand the gravity of the moment. We saw the final soldiers falling from the sky, streaks of metal and flesh, flashing from cloudlet to fire, then disappearing in the city, with only a muffled thump to suggest they had landed.

The Bishop was relieved at first, certain his god had provided rescue. He had found a stone bench outside the cathedral to rest, calling to his Acolyte to bring him a cup of water. I don't know where the boy went, towards the river, perhaps, although there were surely water sources in the city, if they still functioned.

"Not safe, sir. I'm sorry." Song's regret softened her words.

"How?" I couldn't say more. Did I want to

know? I didn't, but this I had to hear.

"Inside a building, sir. They disappeared before Sister's comm went silent. I hoped for Franklin, but sometime after, the building came down, and I knew I would hear nothing else."

"I'm sorry you had to see them go." I looked outside, the street filled with broken buildings quiet for a time. I was certain the ship overhead could pick out our heat signatures even inside our berms of brick and steel. I wasn't hopeful for my long-term prospects at making a break for safety. The image of the Bishop's final moments washed my thoughts before I could push it away. He had stood to greet an approaching soldier, smiling in gratitude for his arrival, and the armed man had lifted his weapon. The holy man had fallen, slumped against the bench he'd just arisen from. The soldier held out a recording device, scanned the Bishop's face, nodded, and turned and walked away.

I had seen the uniform. Army. I hated to think my trust in Recon, Ghost, and Pyro had been misplaced. Surely they were not part of this, but the truth bled all over me. The damage to the *Roosevelt*. Our diversion to Verboten. The hatred I'd seen on the men's faces.

Betrayal was the hot end of an energy weapon burning though my soul, but what was done couldn't be undone.

"Song, are you still there?" I needed to hear her voice.

"Yessir. I see targets in the distance. I have a weapon, sir, and I'm going to make use of it." A cough broke over the comm. "My body! How can this hurt so much? Captain, I'm not making it one way or the other, so I'm taking out as many of them as I can on the way. I hope you make it, sir."

Before I could respond, I heard a door slam open, Song let out a yell, and her energy weapon engaged. I leaned my head against the wall and listened as tears ran down my face. Eventually I realized the comm was silent, and I pulled it from my collar and tossed it aside. There was no one else, except the Android. He was more capable than any other member of my crew. If he needed my help, then it was certain everything was lost.

Noise outside got my attention, and I pulled myself forward to observe the scene. Two soldiers, one with a shock of blond hair and another with dark stood in one of the upper story rooms that had been sliced half away. The one with blond hair bent his knees then leaped, hitting the ground in a crouch and looking around before standing. What was there for him to look for, I wondered. By Song's report, there was no one to oppose them.

Then I caught a silver-black blur, a spinning dervish of blinding quickness. It stirred debris as it whipped onto the scene, and it paused in front of the blond-haired soldier, a central mass with multiple arms ending in three-pronged fingers. They buzzed with electricity. Android, good for you, I thought. One of the three-fingered hands wrapped the man's face, his body convulsed, and the Android became a blur again, with only rising dust to reveal its passage. The dark-haired soldier above was still raising his weapon, and the Android was already gone. The blond man slumped in his exoskeleton, held in place by the mechanical device. His companion leaped to his side, sending dust flying, and began to drag the fallen man toward a broken and shadowy doorway.

If only I had a weapon. I looked around the room I was in, desks and cabinets, some sort of office. I could hardly fight with a chair. Outside, the fallen man's weapon lay canted on the pavement, dropped just outside the shadowed doorway.

I could do this. I had fulfilled my military duties, although decades before. The lessons, the skills I'd acquired were at my fingertips, suddenly fresh in this deadly situation. Make a weapon, any weapon, out of what was available. Just as on the *Roosevelt* when a broken beam had served as a tool to break through the floor, I would have a weapon in my hands; and once across the street . . . *Song,* I thought, *I'll make you proud of me.*

My building, as were most in the city by now, was partially destroyed, and in another room, I found the weapon I needed. A broken beam, much like from the *Roosevelt,* found its way into my hand. I hefted it, a club of steel, bent at the end, perfect for crushing a knee or a skull, if that's where the next few minutes took me.

From outside the building, fresh weapons fire and the electric hiss and crackle of a ship's approaching ARD told me the vessel of death—not to save us but to wreak havoc on a world already known for gifting death to everyone that walked its surface—was here to finish what needed to be done.

Hefting my sledgehammer of a weapon, I moved to the door. Outside, the sky had taken on a red hue, the final heartbeat of a day filled with death. My ship, now my crew and friends. I intended to ensure I gave what payback I could.

With a roar, and my newfound weapon held over my head, I ran into the street, my eyes focused on the blond soldier's energy weapon, determined to make it my prize. I was Captain Vicente Falco, and I intended to be the storm that would make them regret ever placing a booted foot onto the soil of Verboten.

CASK

—Chapter 33—

Interdicted Colony World *Verboten*

Envoy

. . . in which betrayal overtakes everything

THE FIRST THE ENVOY KNEW of the mission's impending peril was a surge of energy from a physical link with the Android. Crippled, the lone surviving representative of the best Earth had to offer performed a Data Dump, wishing to absolve the crew of the *Roosevelt* from complicity in the disaster that had overtaken them. The death of the Earth humans aboard the *Roosevelt* rested on its shoulders. Do not give up hope for a rescue.

Absorbed and processed in its reduced state, the Cygnian accepted the truth with a Zen-like quality of understanding. Not all of Humanity wished for peace. Still, it called to anyone that might be listening that peace, peace was its race's wish for the future. When the Cask's functional level dipped into distress, and alternating pain and fear took over, the Envoy searched the Android's download, hoping to uncover where it had failed. Piecing together the information revealed the betrayal of those most trusted to give the humans support and protection.

The Envoy withdrew into itself, understanding that without the continued assistance of the Cask, it would soon expire, having failed in its mission. It was inconsolable in its despair.

CASK

Chapter 34

Interdicted Colony World *Verboten*

Conclusion
. . . during which all is explained

IN THE DISTANCE, the *Vladimir Vladimirovich Putin* fell from the sky amid the blue glow of its Antigravity Repulsion Device, useful on worlds where there was an innate magnetic field, and this world's was massive. Attitude jets flared, and underneath the vessel, beams of red light flashed out, striking at anything that moved. Only specially outfitted military ships had ARDs powerful enough to maneuver safely within this world's gravity well, something the three soldiers sent to guard the Cask had unwittingly put to their advantage. The wrecked vessel *Roosevelt* lay crumpled in the distance, the mute evidence of an insurgence by the military men sent to ensure the ship's safety and a testament to their preparedness and skill. As the fresh and undamaged vessel landed, a fully suited team outfitted with full atmospheric shielding emerged. The air was just toxic enough that prolonged survival for anyone unmodified was impossible without protection. They located the remains of the *Roosevelt*'s crew and passengers scattered about, some crumpled from the poisoned air and the rest dead or dying, and finished the job. The Android, cursed malleable atrocity that it was, eluded them the longest, but not even a machine could disappear forever.

They located the Cask in the remains of the crippled city, now blasted to broken stumps by the red lasers, and the Android, its state-of-the-art liquid-metal body brutally battered and now damaged beyond any reasonable attempt at retaliation, was plugged in, repeating the Envoy's final words to no one at all, "I was so looking forward to visiting Earth . . ." and going on to describe the Envoy's quashed hopes for a lasting and glorious peace between its home world and the people of Earth. An ominous weapon in gleaming pseudo metal touched the Android's slagged temple and put an end to the final playing card in this dangerous and troublesome debacle.

Then the lone remaining light on the Cask blinked out.

"Bring me McAvoy, Hernandez, and Nissen." Recon, Ghost, and Pyro, the General meant, even if he didn't know those names. "I need to know if they survived."

The versatile Android had been the one wild card they hadn't expected, and the General's hopes weren't high. He stood with his hands behind his back, his voice hard, and his eyes even harder. When the broken soldiers were laid out before him, their face masks shattered and their suits in tatters, his folded leather features softened for a moment, murmuring, "Men, to give your lives to further our cause makes you heroes. We can now get back to our war."

His face turned hard again as the military team gave their three Army comrades a military burial with honors as fallen brothers in combat, while they left the others where they lay.

The *Vladimir Vladimirovich Putin* burned blue, its ARDs generating enough power to run a small moon, as it rose from the massive planet, before winking into the darkness of space, exiting a sky quickly going dusty and red.

See more books by Farley L. Dunn at

Three Skillet Publishing.

www.ThreeSkilletPublishing.com

 THREE SKILLET

www.ingramcontent.com/pod-product-compliance
Lightning Source LLC
Chambersburg PA
CBHW070853250626
47159CB00003B/1051